THE CHRISTMAS HOLIDAY

A totally gripping psychological thriller with a
shocking twist
Mikayla Davids

For my Mum and Dad

Prologue
Now

I trudge through the snow, my breath coming out in puffs, visible in front of me in the frosty air. I scan the hazy horizon but I can barely see anything past the end of my own outstretched hand.

My feet sink into the clean snow. There are no other footprints, no one else has been here for some time. So where is everybody? How have I managed to get so lost?

I keep walking, slow, heavy steps. My boots are dragging me down and my body aches with the effort it takes to keep going. I can't stop, I need to get back to the lodge, otherwise I'll freeze to death out here.

The snow is coming down hard now and, just as I start to despair, I see a light in the distance. It must be the holiday lodge where I'm staying. It has to be.

I stumble forward, eager to get inside, to find warmth. But then I see something in the snow, just ahead of me. Something still and unmoving. It's unmistakeable.

A body.

Spread out like a snow angel, hair fanning out across the white, soft blanket beneath it. A trickle of bright red blood from mouth to cheek, frozen in a moment of time. It looks unnatural – someone has positioned the person in exactly this way to make a statement.

That's when I hear the sirens. The blue flashing lights come closer. And then the German shepherd Garda dogs rush towards me, followed by the shouts of men in uniform.

They speed closer, the gap between us narrowing by the second. I'm clearly the target but, any minute now, they're also going to spot the lifeless shape on the ground in front of me.

They will find me.

And they will find the dead body.

Chapter One

Alicia

I breathe in and out deeply, trying to calm my nerves. This journey has been so long and I can't wait to fold myself out of the car and stretch my aching muscles, but I'm also apprehensive about what I have to face when we reach our destination. I shift in my seat, my legs feeling heavy from sitting in the same position for such a long time. Restless, I try to distract myself by looking at the view around me.

I've never been to Ireland before and I'm in awe of the majesty of the mountains and the vastness of the landscape. The scenery outside is totally mesmerising. I press my nose up to the passenger window of the car, trying to drink in every detail. The sky is a spectacular deep red contrasted with an angry purple. The clouds look as though they've been dipped in paint pots and are like nothing I've ever seen. The colours seep down to meet the mountaintops, and I marvel at how the horizon ahead of me looks both impressive and intimidating.

I'm completely out of my comfort zone on this trip; family holidays aren't something I have much experience of. But I'm going to spend Christmas with my new in-laws, who are my family too now that I'm married to Jack Silver. I'm a ball of excited and nervous energy and I'm finding it difficult to remain still in the passenger seat.

My husband, Jack, is driving. It feels like we've been in the car all day; dusk is now upon us, but we've still got the last hour of the journey to go. I glance over at him and a shiver of happiness courses through my body. Jack is incredibly handsome. He has these big, chocolate brown eyes that I could spend all day looking into, a chiselled jaw which currently has just the right smattering of stubble, and an open, happy face that makes me smile every time I look at him.

'Are you okay?' he asks me, not taking his eyes off the curving road.

'Never better.'

I still can't believe that Jack and I are husband and wife. It feels too good to be true. We've known each other since we both first started working in London, on the same graduate scheme for a finance company. Jack excelled and quickly rose up the ranks. I hated the job and left after a year. But we stayed in touch, bumping into each other at work colleagues' parties and heading out of the city on trips to the coast with mutual friends. After a while, we became more than just acquaintances. Throughout our twenties, we had a casual relationship, not quite girlfriend and boyfriend as we'd go through phases of spending weeks in each other's company and then periods of not seeing one another for months.

Then, all of a sudden, things changed. I went travelling for six months and, when I came back, Jack proposed to me hours after I'd arrived back in England. I was stunned. I always thought I was more into him, which was partly the reason for the trip to Thailand when I hit thirty. It was meant to be a chance for me to shake off all the mistakes of my youth and to move onto pastures new. I was unsure at first about Jack's complete change in attitude to our relationship. Friends convinced me he'd missed me whilst I was away and he'd done a lot of growing up whilst I'd been sunbathing on beaches and exploring temples.

I look down at my diamond-encrusted wedding band and the sparkling engagement ring nestled next to it.

I didn't say yes at first, much to my own surprise. We talked things over for a week or so after he got down on one knee; his offer was everything I'd dreamt of but I wanted to be sure he meant it. We went on a number of special dates to our favourite places and my heart melted. A fortnight after returning from my travels he proposed for a second time and I decided to go for it. I said yes to him and put this gorgeous ring on my finger. Jack and I were officially engaged. He was so thoughtful in all the conversations we had afterwards about where to get married and how to set up our lives together, so we moved from being friends with benefits to a fully-fledged couple very quickly. Our engagement was a whirlwind, Jack proposed in April and by October we were married. All of the big moments – hen do, wedding, honeymoon – happened in an enormous, happy rush The last few months have been so busy and this is the first time I've been able to properly reflect on everything that's happened. I lean back against the headrest and close my eyes. Sighing contentedly, I run through a montage of this year's highlights in my mind.

We had a beautiful crisp, clear autumn day for our nuptials and we walked through the gold, orange and red leaves as we left the church where we'd tied the knot. Our wedding day was simply idyllic. We said our vows at the little village church just north of London where everyone in my family has been christened, married and buried. The only sadness was that my parents were no longer alive to be there. They both passed away within a year of each other when I was in my early twenties, closely followed by the tragic death of my best friend. I would have given anything for the three of them to be there at the most important occasion of my life.

After Jack and I said our vows, the wedding party hopped on a red double decker bus and we were transported to a sumptuous, five-star hotel for the celebrations. It was an out-of-this-world experience. Jack's father paid for the hotel and that's when I first realised quite how wealthy his family was, like another level kind of rich. It wasn't something I was necessarily looking for in a partner, but it's certainly a plus. The Silver family's affluence and Jack's high-flying job means I will never have to worry about money again. Although I plan to continue growing my freelance accountancy business, the weight I previously had on my shoulders to earn a decent income to cover the bills is off. Things couldn't be more perfect.

Jack yawns loudly.

I feel bad he has driven all the way from London to North Wales, where he steered the car through winding country lanes and onto the ferry that departed from Anglesey to Dublin. I can't share the load as I've never learnt to drive. I've always lived in big cities with plenty of public transport options and I didn't see the point in taking lessons. Something to add to the list of New Year's resolutions for next year, because, if we're going to be doing this trip regularly, then I'd like to be able to share the driving. Apparently, the holiday lodge the Silver family own is in a remote spot in the Wicklow Mountains and a car is necessary to get around up there. Jack has shown me pictures and it looks dreamy, set against the backdrop of a small woodland with a snow-capped mountain looming in the backdrop.

'Are you tired? Do you need to stop?' I ask my husband.

'No, let's just get there now. We're so close.'

I wouldn't mind another pit stop to refresh myself before we meet his family. But Jack's the one at the wheel, so I nod and agree.

I'm nervous about spending the Christmas holidays with the Silver family, because I haven't really got to know them very well yet. His father, step-mother, brother and sister all came to London and we had a meal together to celebrate our engagement. It was very sweet of them to make the effort to fly over from Ireland. But, apart from that, I've only really seen them for an hour or two here and there, mostly in connection with arranging the wedding. This is going to be a good opportunity to spend some proper time together. Although I'm also aware I need to impress them and make them see why Jack has married me. I feel like there's a lot riding on this trip, it could literally set the tone for my relationship with his in-laws for the rest of our marriage. *No pressure.*

Eventually, we drive up a long, steep gravel pathway, the car bumping over the stones. Outside, the sky is so beautiful, it's breathtaking.

We crest the small hill and, all of a sudden, a building comes into view. The holiday lodge is picturesque and much bigger than I expected it to be. There are pretty fairy lights around the front door and a warm, welcoming glow coming from the windows. The dusting of snow on the roof makes the property look like an image you'd see on a Christmas card.

'Here we are, this is Bartley Lodge.'

'Wow, is this your father's place?' I can barely contain the awe in my voice.

'Sure is.'

'This is massive! When you said a lodge, I was expecting something small and cosy.'

Jack laughs. 'My dad never does anything on a small scale.'

'I'm beginning to realise that,' I chuckle.

'Anyway, there's eight of us staying here. We're going to need the room.'

'Eight of us? I thought there would be seven?' I rack my brains, trying to think who I've missed. There will be me and Jack, of course, Jack's father Patrick, Jack's stepmother Dawn, his brother Ronan, Ronan's wife Yasmin and their baby Lily. Who's the eighth person?

'Dawn's daughter, Zara, will also be spending the holidays with us.'

'Oh, I didn't know that! I haven't got her a Christmas present.' I've spent hours choosing a gift for each member of Jack's family. I wanted to go the extra mile and I thought about each purchase very carefully, so this information has completely thrown me. I can't believe Jack didn't mention that Zara would be staying here over the holidays too.

'Don't worry about it, she won't be expecting anything.'

'We have to get her something, Jack, it would be rude not to. Is there anywhere we can go to grab something? I'm assuming Amazon deliveries don't come out this far?'

'No, I don't think so. Dad has a PO box at the nearest village, but it's literally a post office, a pub and a grocery store. There are some decent shops about ten miles from here. We can suggest a day trip tomorrow if it makes you happy?'

'Yes, that would be good. I don't want to start off on the wrong foot with anyone.'

'Oh and of course there will be Nuala too.'

'Who's Nuala?'

'My dad's dog.'

'Dog? You didn't tell me he had a dog?' My heart sinks, I'm not very good with animals. I didn't have any of my own pets growing up and I'm never quite sure how to interact with them. If I'd known there was going to be a dog staying with us, I would have read up on the breed or done some kind of preparation.

'Didn't I?'

'No, what kind of dog?'

'An Irish wolfhound.'

'A what?' I've never come across an Irish wolfhound before, but it sounds big.

'Are you worried about this?' Jack briefly turns his big brown eyes towards me.

'Of course I am, Jack! This is the first time I'm spending the Christmas holidays with my in-laws. It's a huge deal.'

Jack leans over and quickly kisses my forehead as we stop at some traffic lights. 'No need to stress, it's all going to be fine. Just be yourself.'

Jack doesn't understand that being myself is the thing I'm anxious about. Everyone in Jack's family is uber posh, so I'm concerned that I won't fit in. I've got one week to get to know them properly and I'm feeling the pressure already. The thought that this holiday could determine the relationship with my in-laws for the rest of my married life keeps whirling round in my head. I hope this is going to be a happy Christmas together, the first of many, and one we will all look back on with fond memories.

Surely nothing can go too wrong on a family Christmas holiday?

Chapter Two

Yasmin

'Happy holidays!' Dawn squeals, drawing Alicia into a warm hug. My stepmother-in-law is wearing an over-sized fluffy white jumper which seems to momentarily absorb Alicia's small frame.

I inwardly roll my eyes at Dawn's over-the-top approach to everything and then move forward to greet Alicia and Jack myself. Jack is my husband Ronan's older brother and Alicia is my new sister-in-law. Jack always comes to spend the Christmas holidays at Bartley Lodge with the rest of the family and we get on well. This is Alicia's first holiday with us, I haven't spent much time with her and we haven't seen each other at all since Alicia and Jack's wedding in the autumn.

'Jack! So nice to see you,' I say, as we kiss each other on the cheek.

'How was your journey?' I ask Alicia. I wasn't going to go in for a hug or a kiss as I barely know Jack's new wife, but she has moved her face towards mine and we rather awkwardly end up bumping cheekbones.

Alicia steps back and flushes red, clearly realising her error.

'It was long!' Alicia replies. We all go quiet at this admission and a worried expression washes over her face. 'But the scenery is just amazing.'

'Come in, come in,' Dawn cries, steering Alicia inside the lodge whilst Jack picks up their luggage.

Alicia looks around in wonder at the interior of the luxury holiday home. It's undeniably impressive when you step through the front door. I was only twenty-one when I started dating Ronan Silver. We were both on the same university course and got together in our final year. I've been included in the Silver family's annual Christmas holiday since we started dating. Ten years later and the place feels like a home from home for me. But I vividly remember the first time I came here and I was similarly awed by the sheer space. The property has been built to specification and is designed to include absolutely everything a family holidaying together could wish for. It's ultra-modern and sleek, with enormous floor-to-ceiling windows in every room that look out onto the snow-capped mountains. So much light fills the house and it almost feels as though you are part of the mountainscape, because the incredible views can be seen from every single room.

'Nuala!' Jack's arms are open as the Irish wolfhound flings herself at him. Despite his absence, Nuala clearly hasn't forgotten who Jack is. Her tail is wagging and she's bouncing on her paws. Swiftly, Nuala turns her attention from Jack to Alicia. She sniffs around Alicia's feet and I watch as Jack's wife freezes. She looks unsure and also a little scared. Nuala rears up on her hind legs, slobbering all over the new guest, her way of welcoming this person into her home. Alicia gives a little yelp and takes a few paces backwards, her arms braced in front of her face to shield herself from the attentions of the dog.

'Nuala, down girl,' Dawn commands.

Nuala isn't very obedient though so it takes several repetitions from Dawn before Nuala calms and retreats along the hallway, her tail still wagging wildly.

Alicia appears shaken. She looks to Jack for reassurance, but he seems oblivious as to how uncomfortable Alicia was just then. It instantly makes me curious about their relationship. There's so much I want to find out about Alicia.

'Patrick is just on a work call; he'll be with us soon.' Dawn smiles, her heavily adorned charm bracelet jangling at her wrist. 'Let's go through to the lounge.'

I observe Jack and Alicia having a whispered exchange and Jack points Alicia in the direction of the downstairs bathroom. She kisses him on the lips before she goes, as though she's about to embark on another long journey and they part ways. Jack follows Dawn and I into the kitchen.

'Coffee?' Dawn asks, already firing up the enormous machine that looks as though it's come from one of the most expensive coffee shops you could find.

Jack nods. 'Definitely,' he says, running his hands through his short, styled brown hair. 'I need a hit of caffeine after the journey.'

He pauses and looks around the flawless high-end kitchen, which stretches the length of the back of the house. The light grey units coupled with the white polished worktops and breakfast bar give the space a minimalist feel. Behind each cupboard door is every kitchen gadget you could possibly wish for. And the space opens up to a dining area, with a wooden table as the centrepiece.

'This is new,' Jack says, moving towards the table and running his hand over the smooth finish.

'Ronan's latest project,' I tell him.

Neither Patrick nor Jack are particularly handsy when it comes to home furnishings and design. But Ronan and I have our own property empire. We have a string of houses we rent out to students in university towns, including Oxford, Cambridge and Durham, as well as a couple of exclusive holiday homes across the UK. We've been building our portfolio and Ronan has embraced all elements of the process. He loves creating unique, bespoke pieces of furniture and has honed his carpentry talents over the years. My passion is upcycling antique furniture and our townhouse in Dublin displays some of my favourite creations.

'Impressive,' Jack comments.

'Here's the man himself!' I say, as Ronan enters the room. He's tall and wiry and currently has our eleven-month-old daughter, Lily, balanced on his hip. Lily's cheeks are rosy and chubby. She still looks half-asleep and snuggly with her head laid on Ronan's chest.

'Ronan!' Jack cries and the two brothers half-embrace, with Lily hovering between them.

'How's my little niece?' Jack coos. 'She's grown loads, look how long her legs are now.'

Ronan transfers our daughter into Jack's arms. 'Here you go, sleepy cuddles are the best cuddles. Enjoy!'

Jack holds Lily in the crook of his arm, her round face tipped up towards his. 'She's totally gorgeous,' he says. 'She must get it from her mum because it's certainly not from her dad,' he smiles with a teasing look on his face.

Jack continues to coo and cradle Lily as Dawn begins to pass round the hot, steaming mugs of coffee. I take mine gratefully. Lily woke up several times in the night and I've not had a proper rest in ages. I feel jangly and on edge, the result of months of sleep deprivation.

I stand in front of the expansive window; the shadow of darkness is just starting to creep across the vivid sky outside. The sunset was a canvas of colour but is now gradually beginning to fade. The scene is tranquil and calming and I exhale a breath that I've been holding onto and try to savour the peace. Lily will want feeding and changing soon and we're likely to be up late this evening. Patrick loves to gather his family and drink and talk way into the evening, but also then insists everyone is up early to make the most of the day. I always used to love coming here, but, with Lily's baby rhythms to now consider, being away from home feels more like a challenge than a break.

'I'm just going to check if Alicia knows where we are,' Jack says and disappears into the hallway with Lily still in his arms.

I go and sit down on the low, pale blue sofa with my coffee mug still warming my hands.

Minutes later, Alicia and Jack come into the kitchen.

Alicia's eyes are fixed on Lily, 'She's so sweet!'

'Do you want to hold her?' Jack says, offering Lily up to Alicia.

'Oh, no it's okay.' Alicia shrinks back from him. 'I haven't held many babies.'

'Don't be silly,' Dawn interrupts. 'You need to get some practice in!' She ushers Alicia to sit down on the L-shaped sofa next to me. Dawn takes the still snuggly baby and carefully places her on Alicia's lap. Alicia is sitting stiffly, her arms held at an awkward angle, looking extremely uncomfortable.

'She's heavier than she looks,' Alicia says.

Lily senses the change from the cosy position Jack was holding her in and screws up her features, going completely scarlet.

'Uh, what's she doing? Am I doing something wrong?' There's a note of panic in Alicia's voice.

Lily responds by bawling at the top of her lungs and kicking her chunky legs. I sigh, the illusion of peace now broken. I put down my mug, reach over and pluck Lily from Alicia's arms.

'It's okay, she's not used to strangers,' I explain.

Alicia looks mortified and flushes red. It was honestly a throwaway comment but I've just highlighted Alicia's status as the newcomer to the family and she doesn't look too happy about it. If it were me in her shoes right now, I would have made a light-hearted reply and tried to smooth the situation over. But Alicia just goes quiet, completely out of her depth.

'She'll get used to you soon enough,' Jack breezes, plopping down on the sofa and throwing an arm around his wife's shoulders.

I stand up, rocking and shushing Lily. She's more than agitated now and her high-pitch wail cuts right through me.

'I'm just going to go next door until she's settled down,' I say, my voice coming out harsher than I meant it to. I quickly exit the room and I think I hear Alicia calling, 'I'm sorry,' behind me, but I'm not entirely sure as my daughter's cries are filling my ears.

It was unfortunate that Alicia didn't have Jack's knack with children. But I hope this isn't a taste of things to come with my sister-in-law. She is absolutely not the kind of person I thought Jack would end up marrying; he's so outgoing and she seems like a little mouse in comparison. Their engagement was such a whirlwind and they wed in such haste that I wondered if Alicia could be pregnant, but that wasn't the case. I must try to get to the bottom of what prompted the speedy nuptials this week. So far, I'm not enamoured with my new sister-in-law. But it's not just because of her nervous disposition. I have more than one reason not to like Alicia Silver.

And, if it's up to me, she's not going to last very long as a member of this family.

Chapter Three

Alicia

'There's a coffee for you there, Alicia,' Dawn tells me, filling in the void in conversation after Yasmin made her swift exit from the room.

'Oh, thanks,' I say, hesitating. I've somehow just caused a scene but I did say I didn't want to hold the baby. I don't know the first thing about children.

'Is there something wrong?' Dawn asks when I don't reach for the coffee mug.

'Sorry, I forgot to say, Alicia only drinks decaf.' Jack smacks his forehead with the palm of his hand.

Dawn laughs. 'Come on, Alicia, live a little. You're on holiday.'

'Sorry,' I say apologetically, 'caffeine gives me bad headaches. I'd better give it a miss.'

'It's okay,' Jack reassures, 'I should've said. What do you want instead?' He swipes my drink away, adding, 'I'll have this. I don't think one coffee will be enough for me!'

I watch him rummaging in the kitchen cupboards, searching to find an alternative for me.

'I don't think we actually have anything that's not got caffeine in. Even the green tea is caffeinated.'

'Don't worry,' I say hurriedly. 'I'll have a glass of water, that's fine, thanks.'

Out of the corner of my eye, I detect Dawn pulling a face at Ronan. My cheeks burn. I don't want them to think I'm being awkward, but I know if I drink even a drop of the coffee I'll be up all night with a migraine. If I was a weak-willed sort of person, then I might give in to something like this at the first temptation. But I'm not. I may seem meek and mild on the surface but I have a steely, strong-willed core.

I am, however, utterly embarrassed. I've been so preoccupied with making a good impression that I seem to be doing and saying all of the wrong things. Dawn obviously thinks I'm being completely precious about what I drink and Yasmin has been more than frosty with me since I arrived. She didn't seem to want to say hello, which ended with the two of us bumping heads. And she practically snatched her baby out of my arms and stormed out of the room with the crying child just now. I've been here less than half an hour, how is this going so badly?

It's not the start I was planning on for this holiday but I know I just need to shake myself off and try again. This week is so important to me, it means everything to be able to fit in with Jack's family. My parents were much older parents; my mother was already in her late forties by the time she had me. As they've already passed away, and I'm an only child, I don't have a proper family of my own. Except for a few distant cousins who I see once or, if I'm lucky, twice a year. This lack of close relatives means I'm not well versed in family dynamics. I don't know what the relationship between siblings is really like, let alone sisters-in-law and stepmothers-in-law. I have no blueprint to follow and nothing to refer to. I feel like the newbie in so many ways. I just need to relax and stop piling so much pressure on myself. But I can still hear the baby wailing in the background and I feel so guilty.

'Here you go.' Jack hands me a tall glass of water.

'Thank you,' I say, gulping down the cool liquid. It's instantly refreshing and just what I needed.

'So what's the plan for tonight?' Jack asks.

'We've booked dinner out,' Dawn replies. 'We're going to The Mount, our Christmas tradition. You know how booked up they get. Patrick's PA made the usual reservation for our private dining area.'

'Ace!' Jack says enthusiastically as he drains the second mug of coffee.

I was hoping we might be able to escape up to bed at a decent hour tonight after our long journey. I'm feeling tired and would like a few hours to decompress, but it seems I'm going to have to perk myself up for this evening meal.

Jack gives me a sideways glance and seems to sense what I'm thinking. 'What time is the booking?'

'7.30 p.m.,' Dawn replies.

'Great, that gives us a few hours. I'm going to give Alicia the guided tour and we can go and unpack and get ourselves ready.' Jack reaches for my hand and helps me up from the sofa. 'We'll see you guys in a bit,' he says to Dawn and Ronan. Ronan has already flicked on the enormous TV screen, which takes up almost the entirety of one wall, and he doesn't respond. Dawn gives us both a tight smile. I do a small, silly wave. I don't know why I did it but I couldn't think of anything to say. I feel like such an idiot.

Jack propels me in front of him and I go out of the door in a rush.

And crash, smack bang, into Patrick.

'Oof!' I pretty much bounce off his solid frame and trip backwards. Jack catches me before I fall.

'What the—' Patrick exclaims.

'I'm so sorry!' I squeak. I truly want the ground to swallow me up.

'Dad!' Jack reaches round the side of me to give his father a handshake.

'Hey, that was quite a greeting.' There's a stern look on Patrick's face and I'm sure he would like to say more but stops himself.

'We're just going upstairs to unpack and freshen up before the meal tonight,' Jack explains.

Patrick looks at his watch, 'It's only five o'clock, there's plenty of time for all that.'

'We won't be long. Just want a quick breather as we're beat after travelling.'

Patrick raises his eyebrows. 'You young 'uns don't know the meaning of a long day.'

Jack doesn't respond, but Patrick is already moving past him into the kitchen.

Jack has a somewhat tense relationship with his father. Patrick is typical of the baby boomer generation; he worked hard and did well out of it financially so he was able to play hard too. He seems to have no understanding that the next generation are working just as hard but they're not reaping the rewards in the same way because the world isn't quite as full of the same opportunities as he had in his day.

'Are you okay?' I whisper under my breath.

'Yep, that's just my dad all over,' Jack replies, through gritted teeth.

Jack and I gather the luggage and make our way up the stairs to the bedrooms.

'My room is at the end of the hallway.' Jack nods towards the furthest door.

'This place is huge!'

'There are six bedrooms and all of them have en suites,' Jack tells me.

'Six?'

'Well, we're starting to fill them now. The Silver brood is expanding! Ronan and Yasmin have their own room, baby Lily has the smallest room, Dad and Dawn have the master bedroom and then Zara is in a separate bedroom as well. There's only one room empty,' Jack winks at me. 'I think Dawn is hoping to hear the pitter patter of tiny feet soon to fill the final room. We'll definitely be a full house then.'

That's the second baby comment in the space of an hour. Jack and I didn't talk about having children before we got married. Somehow it never really came up. I guess I assumed that Jack was so carefree that little ones weren't on the agenda for a while or maybe not even at all. I still haven't worked out how I feel about the whole motherhood thing yet. I honestly don't know if it is for me. I've never been naturally maternal and I haven't spent a lot of time around kids. But Jack keeps dropping hints like this without us having had a discussion about it. I need to broach it with him and talk about it properly, but this week certainly isn't the time. Another thing to add to my list for the new year.

I gape as we enter the room allocated to us. 'Wow, this is incredible!'

'It's not bad, is it?'

There's a four-poster bed in the centre of the room. The colours are neutral, beiges and whites and soft hues. Everything is so tastefully decorated. Like the rest of the house, it's all very minimalist. There's a discreet sliding door set into the far wall that I guess is the wardrobe and there's also another door, which must be to the en suite. It all seems very surreal; somehow I've managed to step into this world of luxury and decadence like Alice falling down the rabbit hole.

'This is the en suite.' Jack points through the now open mystery door after he's dumped the bags on the floor.

I peek my head around the corner. The bathroom is equally lush, with a double shower and a huge claw-foot bath. My eyes pop at the sight. 'Oooh, that bath!'

'I can confirm it is just as relaxing as it looks. Perhaps we can both try it out later...' Jack gives me a suggestive look.

I blush. I'm still not used to him focusing all of his attention on me like this. Before my trip to Thailand, which was less than a year ago, we enjoyed each other's company, but Jack never seemed to take our connection seriously. This new side to him still gives me butterflies.

We kiss, slowly at first and then with more heat. I pull away before we get too carried away.

'What's the matter?' Jack asks.

I shake my head to indicate nothing's wrong, hooking a strand of my strawberry blonde hair behind my ear.

'I mean, are you okay being here, with my family?'

'Of course,' I say automatically.

'It's probably a bit overwhelming. Maybe we should have had our first Christmas at home, by ourselves.'

'No, of course not. I'm glad to be here. It's a great chance to get to know your family.'

My husband hugs me and kisses the top of my head.

I think of our lovely apartment back in London. It's in a serviced building that has its own pool and gym and it's right by a tube station. It's a two-bed flat with two reception rooms. It's nothing in size in comparison to this holiday house, but it's more than I ever dreamt I'd be able to afford. We were only able to purchase the well-appointed apartment because Patrick contributed a hefty amount to the deposit as a wedding present. It was more than generous and it means we've been able to start our married life off in a comfortable home. I'm so thankful to Patrick for his support, so I feel guilty that I really would rather be back in London in my own marital bubble than here, with Jack's family. I'm sure it's just because I'm anxious. Hopefully, I'll start enjoying myself soon.

'So what's the dress code for tonight?' I ask.

'Smart casual.' Jack shrugs flippantly, as he unzips his suitcase.

It's all very well for guys, a shirt and chinos will do in most situations but smart casual covers a whole spectrum of possibilities for women. I start to unpack my own luggage and wonder what I should wear. I'm keen to fit in and impress, so I lay out two choices on the bed. One option is a shimmery pair of trousers with a loose silk blouse, the other is a silver, sparkly body con dress.

'Which do you think?' I ask Jack.

'You'll look beautiful in both,' he replies.

'That's not helpful.' I laugh as he catches my hand and kisses it.

'I might have a quick shower first, hopefully it will wake me up a bit.'

We spend the next half an hour readying ourselves for the evening ahead and I feel more confident with freshly applied make-up. I view myself in the mirror for the final time and take a deep breath. I'm determined that tonight will go well.

I glance down at my emerald cut engagement ring. I wanted Jack Silver more than anything. Now he's mine, I'm prepared to do whatever it takes to make sure it stays that way.

Chapter Four

Jack

I stand in the shower, the hot water coursing over my body. I turn the heat up another notch, so it's verging on scalding, before switching the dial to ice cold. The freezing water sends shockwaves through my skin, jolting me wide awake. The journey here to the holiday lodge in the Wicklow Mountains always feels epic. I was feeling drowsy and tired after the drive, so I needed to take some time to pull myself out of a stupor, ready for the evening ahead. I'm somehow always the last one to arrive at Bartley Lodge, which makes me feel on the back foot. Everyone else has already had a chance to settle in and switch to holiday mode.

Ronan and Yasmin live in Dublin, so it's not too far for them to come and, by the sounds of things, they're back and forth here practically every weekend. Ronan finds it a good place to entertain his friends and Yasmin likes the fresh air and the quiet up here. My father and Dawn don't use the place often; they're based in Dublin but travel a lot for work purposes. My father has been spending a lot of time in Dubai in recent years, so they mainly come to Bartley Lodge for a week or two over Christmas and about the same amount of time in the height of summer. My visits are even less frequent, I rarely come other than for our traditional festive holiday, so I don't feel as in tune or familiar with the place as the others.

I know Alicia is fretting about spending the time with my family and, in turn, this is making me feel tense. I usually just kick back and go with the flow when I'm here. But I'm going to have to make a bit more of an effort this year to help Alicia feel comfortable and included.

As I get ready and slip the thick gold wedding band onto my ring finger, I can't help but marvel at how much has changed in the last year. If anyone had said this time last Christmas that I'd be a married man by the time the festive season rolled around again, I would've laughed in disbelief. Marriage was so far off my agenda a year ago, but a rapid chain of events meant that Alicia and I tied the knot in the autumn. So I'm now someone's husband.

A lot of my friends asked if Alicia was pregnant when we announced we were getting married. I can see why they assumed that. Alicia and I had been seeing each other in a casual, non-committal way for a number of years. We met during a graduate scheme placement, but I forget exactly when we first became lovers. It feels like she's always been part of my life. But the reason for our shotgun wedding was nothing to do with her having a bun in the oven. I don't think I could have coped with going from my easy bachelor lifestyle straight into married life and parenting at the same time. I could see the relief on people's faces when I told them there wasn't a surprise baby on the way, my family included. I haven't exactly been the responsible type to date. Sure, I've held down a good job, but nothing else about the way I've lived my life has been remotely grown-up. I've worked hard, but I've partied harder.

I smooth my hair back and slap on some aftershave before changing speedily into my designer jeans and cream cable-knit jumper. Life so far has been pretty breezy. Which is why, when choosing a wife, I didn't want to tip the balance too much.

I go back into the spacious bedroom and watch Alicia as she finishes brushing her long, shining hair. She picks up a silver necklace and loops it around her neck, struggling with the clasp.

'Here, let me,' I say, crossing the room and deftly securing the necklace in place.

'Thank you,' Alicia says, turning to kiss me.

'You look enchanting.' And she really does. She's wearing a cute silver, glittery dress that hugs her figure in all the right places.

Alicia blushes in response. I take her hand and gently kiss each of her fingers. She shivers.

'What time should we venture back out?' Alicia asks, a questioning look on her face.

'No need to rush, the taxi won't be here for ages.' I pull Alicia close to me and we kiss again, this time with more electricity between us.

Alicia gently pushes me away, 'Don't tease me. We're about to have dinner with your family.' A smile plays over her lips and she turns back to the dressing table and picks up her lipstick.

'We're newly-weds, no one will care if we're a bit late.'

'I'll care.' Alicia applies a peachy-coloured lipstick and pouts.

'Fair enough. But just try to chill a little. They're all human too.' I'm disappointed, but it's sweet that's she's putting so much effort in.

Alicia looks thoughtful and then says, 'It's important to me. I want your family to like me.'

'They do.'

'But I don't really know them yet. I want us all to be a proper family.'

'And we will be,' I reply reassuringly.

Alicia carries on getting ready, dabbing some perfume at her wrists and slipping on her high-heel shoes. This holiday means a lot to her, she wants to fit in. Well, more than that really, she's desperate to fit in. She doesn't have an immediate family of her own anymore and seems to have this idea of a big, happy family that is based on wholesome movies and not at all rooted in reality. Her own family set-up was pretty simple, two loving parents and an only child. Mine is very different. It's all kinds of complicated. I've tried to hint at this to Alicia, to manage her expectations, but she's so focused on this dream of what family life will be like that I can't shatter her illusions this early on.

I just hope everyone behaves themselves. Dawn doesn't really engage her brain before she opens her mouth and says exactly what she thinks. My stepsister, Zara, despite being a similar age to me, is like a moody, petulant teenager when she's around the rest of the family. On her own, she's more down-to-earth and hides a wicked sense of humour behind her moody exterior but most of the time she just comes off as being rude. Dad and Ronan usually stray into talking business whenever they're together. And Yasmin is completely wrapped up in her baby at the moment. She used to be fun, the person who lifted these family gatherings, but she looked tired today and lately she only has eyes for little Lily.

I'm going to have to try to make Alicia's first Christmas with us feel special for her whilst also navigating the tensions that run deep in the family. I'm exhausted just thinking about it. At least Alicia is pretty low-maintenance. She may get nervous about certain social situations, but, on the whole, she's not demanding in the way that some women I've dated have been. I guess that was part of the appeal. Alicia has always seemed happy just to be around me. We were never officially boyfriend and girlfriend, but she was keen to hang out, to slot into my life in a way that I took for granted. My mates would joke that she was a wife-in-waiting. In the end, they were right. But it took Alicia going travelling for six months to push me into recognising that I wanted her in my life more permanently. I realised I didn't want her to slip through my fingers. I was relieved when she came back to England, still unattached.

'Ready,' Alicia says, taking my hand. She looks stunning.

I open the door for her in a gentlemanly way and we head back downstairs. I have everything crossed that tonight goes well. I want my family to like her too. I married Alicia for many reasons. Because she's amenable, easy-going and pretty. And because I know she loves me. But, the truth is, I don't really love her. Not properly. I appreciate her and, maybe, in time, true love will happen for us. But there was another reason I married Alicia. A reason far more pressing than love or the need for companionship. And I need to make sure she never finds out the real explanation behind why I proposed so suddenly and then insisted on a short engagement, followed by a sprint to the altar.

There are only two people who know why I married Alicia. I'll do whatever it takes to protect that truth. I need my new wife to believe this marriage is forever so that the plan I've set in motion goes without a hitch.

Otherwise, saying 'I do' will be the worst mistake of my life.

Chapter Five

Yasmin

Lily won't stop crying. I've tried everything. She doesn't want to feed, her nappy is clean and I've used every trick I know to try to cajole her out of her tantrum, but nothing has worked.

'Lily, please,' I murmur after more than half an hour has gone by. I transfer her to my other shoulder and try patting her back once more.

At that moment, Ronan finally turns up to see what's going on. He must have heard Lily's cries – I'm sure the whole house has – so I'm annoyed he hasn't come to check on us before.

'She won't stop screaming,' I say. I'm agitated now and feeling distressed at my daughter's unhappiness. What if something's wrong? What if she's unwell?

'Come here, baby,' Ronan says, lifting Lily out of my arms.

Instantly, she stops wailing.

Ronan grins widely. 'She just wanted her daddy, didn't you, Lil.' He blows a raspberry on her wet cheek and she giggles.

I throw my hands in the air in despair. 'Seriously! I'm beginning to think she just doesn't like me.'

'Don't be daft,' Ronan says, 'she's just got used to me being around more over the last few weeks. We'd better try to tire her out so she sleeps in the pram when we're eating.'

I sigh. Going for a meal that starts at 7.30 p.m. isn't ideal with a baby in tow. If we're lucky, she may be tired enough that she sleeps through everything, but, given she's a light sleeper, I'd be astonished if that actually happens. It's more likely that she'll be grisly at being out of her routine. I'm not looking forward to the dinner, and we haven't even gone out yet.

I contemplate suggesting to Ronan that he goes out for the meal while I stay here with Lily. Except, I'm certain of his answer before I've even asked. He will want us all to go as a family and also for his Dad and Dawn to have the opportunity to see more of Lily. It's just a shame that neither of them will volunteer to bounce her up and down on their knees and help to entertain her. I'm sure Lily will end up attached to me as I attempt to snatch cold forkfuls of my food.

It also doesn't help that if I said I was staying at the lodge so the baby could sleep in her cot, Dawn would scold me for being too obsessed about Lily's routine. She's already reminded me at least five times since we got here a few days ago that she never changed her life to fit around Zara and her daughter accompanied her to all sorts of events and social gatherings when she was younger. I've had to bite my tongue hard not to retaliate by saying that I definitely don't want Lily to grow up to be anything like brooding, sullen-faced Zara.

'I'm knackered after all of that crying, so I expect she will be too,' I snap, feeling irritable now. 'I'm going to go and lay down for half an hour before we go out.'

Ronan looks a bit taken aback. 'Oh, okay.'

'You'll be fine with her for thirty minutes.'

'Yeah, I'll play with her for a bit,' he says uncertainly. Despite him being around a bit more in the last few weeks, he tends to flit in and out of Lily's vision, giving kisses here and cuddles there, but not in a way that's consistent or part of her routine. He's usually only around for the good bits – I'm praying that this holiday might make him realise there's more to parenting than giggles and hugs. Maybe he might start stepping up a bit more.

I go to leave the room but I'm called back instantly.

'What is it?'

'She was reaching out for you,' Ronan says as Lily stretches out her chubby hands in my direction as if she's demonstrating on demand.

I look at my little daughter and my heart leaps. I'm about to take her back from Ronan but I strengthen my resolve. I kiss Lily on the top of her cute button nose. 'Daddy wants a cuddle,' I tell her.

Lily nestles into Ronan's chest and he looks both surprised and delighted at the display of affection from someone so tiny.

I creep back out of the room, expecting to hear a fresh burst of tears from Lily. But they don't come. All is quiet, so I escape while I can.

I plod upstairs, sink into the soft, luxurious bed and rest my aching body. I absorb the room and my plush surroundings before switching off the light. We've spent so much time at Bartley Lodge in the last year that I had the room redecorated at the start of December, just in time for this holiday. It still feels fresh and new. The rich, high-end curtains perfectly match the lavish bedspread. The natural tones in the room, complete with trailing plants, make the space feel calm, which is exactly what I need right now.

As I pull the warm covers over me, my mind is whirring. I'm sure Ronan will play with Lily for all of five minutes and then pass the baby over to Dawn. He loves our daughter, but he's got a short attention span where she's concerned. I'm hoping when she gets a bit more interactive he might start taking more of an interest. I can't think about all of that though, I just want to close my eyes and drift off for a few blissful minutes. Whoever said sleep deprivation is a form of torture was completely correct, as I'm sure most parents will agree.

All the parenting blogs out there assure me these days will pass and, in the not too distant future, I will be able to sleep through the night once again without multiple wake-ups to change nappies, feed and resettle a baby who hasn't yet managed more than a stretch of four and a half consecutive hours' sleep. I know this, because my smart watch keeps a meticulous record of the sporadic shut-eye that I'm getting along with all of the sleep I'm missing out on.

Even now, as I try to relax, sleep won't come. I'm wide awake and restless. I wriggle and turn onto my side, questions looping round my brain like an annoying stuck record. Have we stocked up on enough milk for the baby? Is she teething? Why is Ronan being so protective of his phone lately? Why, of all people, did Jack choose to marry Alicia?

As I conjure up an image of Alicia, the newest member of the Silver family, a number of unsettling scenarios circle in my mind. As I close my eyes and finally drift off, the last thought I have is: How can I get rid of my sister-in-law?

Chapter Six

Now

How is this happening? I'm standing here, metres away from a dead body. I'm on my own, I've been wandering around in this cold wilderness for at least an hour and I don't have anyone to account for my movements.

This doesn't look good. At all.

One of the German shepherds pulls to a halt by the body that's slowly being covered by the falling snow. The dog barks sharply three times and then sits, as if guarding the prone figure.

What do I do now? Just stand here, waiting for the Garda officers to reach me and face the consequences?

Every fibre in my body is screaming at me to run. To get away from this situation as fast as I can.

This doesn't feel right, I'm not meant to be here. This is the wrong time, wrong place for me in the worst way possible.

But I can't move. I know it won't take much for the dogs and the police to catch up with me. I'm exhausted as it is and I don't have a lot of energy left. I'll also make myself look even more guilty if I flee. So I stand, rigid as a statue, waiting for the inevitable. Waiting for the bite of the handcuffs and the sting of the words from the arresting officers.

I didn't do this.

This had nothing to do with me.

I'm not a killer.

But will they believe me?

Chapter Seven

Alicia

'Ah, there they are!' Patrick claps his big hands together and nods towards Jack as he reaches the bottom of the stairs. Dawn, Ronan, Yasmin and Lily are clustered in the hallway behind him, boots and coats on, ready for the outing. 'Is everyone here now?' Patrick booms, to no one in particular.

I hover on the stairs, feeling embarrassed once again. I hadn't anticipated everyone waiting around for us. Jack seemed to think the meal would be a leisurely affair but I have no idea what to expect. I can feel several sets of eyes on me, as though I'm being assessed, and I feel uncomfortable at the attention. I hope I've picked the right outfit and that it's not too over-the-top. Dawn and Yasmin both have their coats on already, so I can't tell if my silver dress is striking the right note for this evening or not.

I wonder how we will get to the restaurant and how long it will take us, given the weather. I shouldn't be surprised to find out that it's all in hand – I hear Dawn saying Patrick's PA has organised taxis to take us there and back. As we go outside, I notice the snow has stopped falling, so the world appears still and white and clear. It's as if Patrick's PA has arranged the weather for us as well. It seems that my father-in-law's life runs like clockwork, thanks to the mystery woman who manages his diary.

'Zara is just coming,' Dawn says.

The rest of us pile outside and into the two awaiting taxis. One is a four-seater and one is a six-seater. Yasmin and Ronan go in the four-seater, which has a baby seat in place for Lily. Jack and I pile into the six-seater car, followed by Patrick and Dawn.

'Where is that girl?' Patrick barks.

'I'll go and find her.' Dawn slides back out of the taxi and hurries into the lodge.

'She's going to make us all late,' Patrick huffs.

A few minutes of awkward silence ensues. Jack is looking out of the window, seemingly unaware of the tension. The taxi with the others moves off down the sloping driveway. Patrick becomes more and more restless, checking his flashy watch and glaring towards the front door. I stay quiet as I don't know Patrick well enough to try to smooth things over.

'Ah! Finally,' Patrick scowls..

'Here she is,' Dawn says in a sing-song voice that feels too bright and jolly for Patrick's current mood.

Dawn sits back down next to Patrick, in the middle seat, and Zara squashes into the seat beside her. I see a flash of dark hair and dark clothing but I don't want to stare too much. So I busy myself by clipping my seat belt firmly in place. I look towards Jack, who still has his gaze fixed on the winter-wonderland scenery outside his window. I peer over his shoulder. The lodge looks perfect with the dusting of snow on its rooftop, a cute little wreath hanging on the door and miniature Christmas trees complete with fairy lights on either side of the door.

It's clear my husband isn't going to introduce me to Zara, who I've only met fleetingly. She was at our wedding, but on the day she was a figure on the periphery and I didn't have a chance to say hello to her. She came to the service and sat through the wedding breakfast but I guess she must've slipped away fairly soon after that. I didn't really register her presence as there was so much going on. The whole day was such a joyful blur. I'm looking forward to getting the professional photographs back as well as the video of our big day, so I can properly soak up the details.

I look at the young woman sitting across from me and, with a jolt, I realise her face is very familiar. I'm sure I must know her from somewhere, but I can't quite put my finger on where. Or perhaps it's just that she looks like someone I've had a passing acquaintance with before. I wrack my brains, trying to work out if there is a connection between us or if she is indeed a doppelganger of somebody that I used to know, but my brain fails to come up with an answer.

Zara is now glaring back at me and I'm aware I've been scrutinising her for a full minute now. She must wonder why I'm ogling her.

'Hi,' I say a little breathlessly. 'I'm Alicia, it's lovely to meet you properly.'

Jack's eyes swivel towards us.

Zara doesn't respond.

'Do I know you from somewhere?' I say in a rush. 'Sorry, I was staring a bit because I swear I've met you – or someone very like you – before.'

She frowns at me and remains tight-lipped. All of a sudden, I feel very claustrophobic in the small space of the taxi and, for a horrible minute, it looks as though Zara isn't going to reply.

'I don't think so,' she finally says.

'You must have a twin out there then!' I give a false laugh. 'It'll come to me at some point.'

Zara gives me a blank look. She clearly doesn't want to make small talk.

Is it me? Have I said something wrong? Or does she just not want to be going out this evening?

'Oh, we must try to work it out!' Dawn swoops in, filling the pause in conversation. 'Perhaps you two have crossed paths before, it's a small world after all.' Dawn gives me an encouraging smile. 'Where did you grow up, Alicia?'

'In a village just north of London.'

Dawn chuckles. 'Well, that doesn't narrow it down much! Although Zara grew up in Essex, so it's unlikely you would've met each other as children.' Dawn looks thoughtful and then continues, 'You work in London, is that right?'

I nod in response, but before I can say anything, Zara cuts in.

'Oh Dawn, just stop. We don't know each other, okay?'

I'm taken aback by this sharp outburst from Zara and I really wish I'd never said anything now. But how was I to know that she'd be so stroppy?

'It's okay, it's probably just my poor memory.' Another false laugh from me. This is super embarrassing.

Our little group descends into silence again and, for the next ten minutes, I try not to look in Zara's direction. It's pretty difficult, though, as she's sitting right opposite me. Zara's hair is so dark that it looks almost blue. After a few discreet glances, I realise that it's not a trick of the light and that she does have blue highlights running through her long locks and the ends of her hair look as though they've been dipped in a pot of midnight blue paint. Her dark hair hangs heavily around her petite face, contrasting against her pale skin. She is wearing a bomber jacket, jeans and chunky boots – her whole outfit is black and, along with her dark eyeliner and mascara, she looks brooding and edgy. Her look is completed with silver-painted fingernails and a thick silver belt at her waist. She also has a number of piercings, including a lip piercing, a nose piercing, as well as several silver hoops in each ear. I could never look that cool and Zara seems to give off an air of effortlessness as well as an air of disdain, although I'm not sure if that's her usual attitude or whether this is just her response to me this evening.

I wonder why Zara didn't refer to Dawn as 'Mum', but calling her mother by her first name seems to fit Zara's personality somehow.

She catches my eye again and I look away hastily, reaching for Jack's hand next to me and giving it a squeeze in the hope that he might strike up a different line of conversation and shake away the weird atmosphere in the back of the cab.

But, in the end, it's not my husband that comes to the rescue, it's the taxi driver.

'You folks should have a good evening at The Mount, the Christmas decorations there look even better than last year!' His Irish lilt feels comforting after Zara's clipped tone. 'Are you still wanting a pick-up at eleven p.m.?' the driver continues.

'Oh yes, that would be wonderful,' Dawn chirps.

'Well, if you want picking up sooner, just give me a call,' the driver says. 'The snow is meant to start falling heavier around ten p.m., so I wouldn't want you to get snowed in.'

'Snowed in? Do you think it will come to that?' Dawn asks.

'Looking at those clouds, I reckon we'll all be snowed in for the next few days. Definitely a white Christmas this year.'

'It's a good job we booked our table tonight then, otherwise we would have missed our opportunity,' Dawn muses.

'I hope you've got enough supplies in?' the driver asks.

'We have, thank you,' Dawn responds evenly.

Patrick's expression shows he's unimpressed by the driver's opinions.

'Have you been to this restaurant many times before?' I ask politely, stepping in to try to defuse the situation.

'Oh yes,' Dawn replies before Patrick can say anything. 'It's a favourite of ours. The Mount is a Christmas tradition, we always have a meal there in the lead-up to Christmas.'

'Best restaurant I've ever been to,' Patrick chips in. 'We're not cutting our evening short just for a bit of snow!'

'It'll be more than a bit, I can tell you,' the driver retorts. 'I know these mountains like the back of my hand and we won't be able to move anywhere by tomorrow morning.'

Patrick harrumphs at this. He says in a loud whisper to Dawn, 'This guy just wants to clock off early.' We all, of course, hear his complaint, including the man at the wheel of the car.

'I can assure you that's not the case,' the driver says, his accent thickening. He's pissed off now and I don't blame him. Patrick has been downright rude; the poor man was only trying to give some advice. 'I'll be with you for eleven p.m. But just be warned it may be a longer journey back.'

The radio flicks on and the driver makes it clear that's the end of that conversation.

Jack looks over at me and it seems he finally notices how uncomfortable I am. He starts to give a detailed overview of the menu and his favourite dishes. Dawn joins in, eager to give her recommendations to me as well, followed by Patrick, who also chimes in with his own thoughts.

I'm relieved the discussion takes an upward turn and, the closer we get to the restaurant, the happier everyone appears to be.

All except Zara.

Perhaps everyone has just got a bit hangry, that can turn even the easiest of situations sour.

I also feel my own mood lifting and I'm excited to see the restaurant that Jack's family have praised so much. My mouth is watering a little bit too. It's been a long day and I haven't eaten a lot, so I'm looking forward to a good meal.

The car jerks without warning, and I clutch Jack's hand a little harder.

'Woah!' Dawn exclaims.

'What was that?' Patrick demands.

'Sorry, folks, the roads have already iced up,' comes the driver's reply over a Christmas song on the radio. 'I did say…'

Patrick chooses to ignore this comment.

'Oooh, we're nearly there,' Dawn announces. 'Not far to go now!'

I exhale deeply. I'll be glad when this car journey has come to an end. I do feel a bit stressed about being on the icy roads late at night, but I try to squash my concerns and concentrate on the aim of the journey.

Tonight should be a happy occasion. A family together celebrating the start of the festivities.

This is my chance to impress the Silver family. I'm not throwing away my shot at charming them. I've come a long way from the day I first set eyes on Jack. After all I've put up with in my quest to become Mrs Silver, I think I deserve an evening of fine dining in a fancy restaurant.

I want us to have the perfect marriage and the perfect life together. And this opulent setting is just the start of things to come.

Chapter Eight

Yasmin

We drive through the gated entrance of The Mount and, even though I've been coming here every Christmas for the last ten years, the sight of the impressive building still takes my breath away. It says something that Patrick feels the same way, and his world is no-expense-spared, so this must be something special. The building curves in a half-moon shape and the whitewashed exterior makes it look as though an architect has lifted this structure from somewhere in Italy or Greece and set it down in the wrong place, here in the Wicklow Mountains where old stone cottages are sprinkled across the rugged countryside.

'We're here, baby,' I whisper to my daughter, who is sleeping soundly in the car seat. She's gently snoring and looks so cute wrapped up in her little snowsuit. I don't want to lift her out of her snug surroundings, but I need to transfer her into the pram that's currently in the boot of the cab. I hope I can get away with moving her without Lily waking up. 'Ronan, can you set the pram up please?'

'Me?' Ronan replies, a look of incredulity on his face. 'I don't know how to set that contraption up at the best of times, let alone when it's snowing.'

I look out of the window and see that he's correct, the snow is coming down harder now. But it's still no excuse, I have to pop the pram up and down several times a day. He should have the hang of it by now. He's making absolutely no attempt to move though, and it's clear I'm going to have to brave the chilly wind that's howling outside.

Pushing down my annoyance, I take off my seat belt and start to extract myself when the driver says, 'Don't worry, love, my granddaughter has the same model. I'll have the pram up for you in no time and then you can get that sleeping beauty into the warm as fast as possible.'

'Thank you,' I say, appreciating his thoughtfulness. If only Ronan was this attentive.

'Nice one,' Ronan adds, clearly relieved not to have to faff about in this weather.

'You really need to master the knack of that pram, you know.'

'She'll grow out of it soon enough.' Ronan's reply is simple and dismissive.

'Yes, but what about when the next one comes along?'

Ronan turns to me eagerly then. 'Of course, you're right, I need to learn.' He pauses, his eyes shining with hope. 'Do you think you might be pregnant again then?'

Ronan and I have been trying for another baby for the last couple of months. I can't say my mind or my body feels ready to have another child just yet, but Ronan is keen to have our children close together so there isn't a big age gap. This is all because he already has grand plans for our retirement, once he's packed Lily, and any other siblings, off to university or whatever path they might follow once they've finished school. He doesn't want to be an older parent. Although I do see the sense in the argument of getting all the sleepless nights and toddler tantrums out of the way in one go, it feels far from a sensible choice right now.

'I was going to tell you later, but I'm just over two weeks late on my period. So potentially...'

Ronan whoops with delight.

'Sssh,' I say, looking furtively out of the window. 'I'm not certain yet, it might just be lack of sleep knocking my hormones out of whack.'

'But you're usually pretty regular, aren't you?'

I smile in response. 'I am, so it's possible.'

Ronan grins and reaches over to place his hand on my stomach. 'Just think, we could have a son growing inside you right now.'

'Let's not be too hasty,' I tell him. 'I want to do a test to see what it says before we go jumping to conclusions.'

'How do you feel?' Ronan asks me. 'Do you *feel* pregnant?'

I consider his question. I don't really remember what those first few weeks with Lily were like, it seems such a long time ago now.

'I think I started feeling queasy with Lily around eight weeks, but maybe it was earlier...' I trail off, thinking back to the excitement of discovering I was going to be a mother for the first time. My heart leaps; I feel equally joyful at the thought of a second child blooming inside me.

'Maybe you don't feel sick yet because it's a little boy. Isn't that the old wives' tale? Girls make you feel sick and boys don't?'

I'm not surprised that Ronan has stored this nugget away. He's openly obsessed with the idea of having a male heir, a son who might follow in his footsteps. It's such a traditional view to hold and I've told him, time and time again, that Lily could take up the helm and run his business when she's older. But he's also let me in on his daydreams of playing footie with a little boy and taking him to watch stadium matches. Again, I've reminded him that Lily may want to do both of those things when she grows up, but my husband has clearly learnt to stereotype males and females from his old-fashioned father. My husband certainly has a lot of ingrained ideas for me to try to unpick if I want to try and bring Ronan's views on children into the century we're actually living in.

'All sorted,' the driver informs us, opening my car door and letting in an icy blast of air.

Ronan quickly steps out of the car, leaving me to carefully inch the sleeping baby out of her seat. I transfer Lily to my shoulder and deftly manage to get her into her pram. I make sure the rain cover is firmly in place over her carriage, without waking her. A wave of relief washes over me; if she stays sleeping I might be able to relax a bit during this meal.

'That was expertly done!' the driver says with a kind smile.

Ronan is standing at my elbow, impatient to be inside. We say our thanks and rush towards the inviting building in front of us. The hedgerow either side of the pathway leading up to The Mount is adorned with sparkling lights and the archway over the door looks very festive, with more pretty lights weaved around a natural-looking green garland with pine cones.

A doorman is awaiting us and helps us get the pram up the steps and inside the building.

'Welcome,' he greets us. 'Let me take your coats.'

We hand over our wet outer layers.

'Have a wonderful evening,' the doorman adds before departing for the cloakroom.

We proceed to the reception area, where we see the clean, shiny desk is complete with a miniature Christmas tree and there's a larger one off to the side, shimmering with pretty ornaments.

'Good evening,' the receptionist greets us with a friendly expression. 'I'm delighted to welcome you to The Mount. Can I check what name the booking has been made under?'

'Silver,' Ronan steps forward, puffing his chest out somewhat and showing a display of pride at his family name.

'Ah, yes, of course. It's fantastic to have you dining with us again.'

I'm sure that Patrick's PA has impressed upon the management how her boss expects to be treated. To be fair, we've never had anything but excellent service from the staff here. Which is part of the appeal for Patrick. And there's no denying Ronan revels in it too. He's definitely his father's son.

'Come through and I'll get you seated.' The receptionist guides us into the main dining room, which is surprisingly busy given the poor weather outside. The tables are set spaciously apart and I'm able to glide Lily's pram effortlessly past the other diners. The receptionist gestures to a large circular table that's by the window, at the far end of the room, behind a small partition wall. This is Patrick's favourite private dining spot and we've been seated here on multiple occasions over the years.

I sit down in the seat I usually take, which has a wonderful view of the grounds of The Mount. Darkness has already descended, but I'm familiar with the layout of the gardens that extend into the distance. The restaurant is part of a hotel and spa. There's an eighteen-hole golf course here and even a gorgeous secluded secret garden, all set against the backdrop of the mountains beyond.

I always get a sense of déjà vu whenever I come here and, as this is a yearly ritual, I often wonder what life will be like in a year's time when I take my place at the table once more. This moment has also become an opportunity for reflection on the year gone by as well. This time last year, Lily hadn't been born. Her first birthday is just a month away and, twelve months ago, I was at this very table in the last trimester of pregnancy. I remember not really being able to eat much as my baby was positioned high up. It felt as though she was pressing on my ribcage and as a result my appetite was largely reduced. I intend to make up for it tonight.

Ronan takes my hand from his seat beside me. 'Last December you were ready to pop with Lily.'

It's rare that my husband and I have the same thought processes, so I'm happy that his train of thinking is similar to mine for once.

'I know – how life has changed since then!' My laughter is light and teasing. Life really has changed a huge amount, in ways that I never imagined possible. My daughter and her well-being are the centre of my universe at all times. I never thought I'd get quite so wrapped up in the baby bubble, but I've been totally sucked in and I really wouldn't want it any other way.

'And baby number two might be cooking away in there right now.' Ronan lays his hand lovingly on my stomach again.

I'm pleased he's so thrilled at the prospect I might be pregnant, but I'm also feeling wary about celebrating too soon. I need to take a test to be sure. I regret mentioning my inkling now as I know my husband has a tendency to run away with an idea that he's excited about.

'Maybe, but let's not get too carried away. I want to be certain.'

Ronan nods in a way that makes me think what I'm saying is going in one ear and out the other.

'Don't say anything to the others,' I implore him. 'We need to check if my hunch is right first.'

Just then, Patrick and Dawn appear in our cosy space with Zara, Jack and Alicia just behind them.

'We made it!' Patrick says in his booming voice. 'Despite our cab driver being a moron.'

'Patrick!' Dawn giggles. 'Don't be so harsh on the man!'

'It's true, trying to spook us all about the weather. As if we haven't spent a winter here before. We're not tourists, you know.'

Dawn giggles again and flaps a hand in Patrick's direction in a gesture. 'Let's not talk about it anymore, we made it here and that's the main thing.'

Zara slips by Dawn and sits down at the round table, with her back to the window. Dawn and Patrick have been married for five years now and Zara has joined us for the last three Christmases in Ireland. With the addition of Lily's bulky pram and another seat needed for Alicia this year, the private dining area we're in is starting to feel more cramped. If Ronan and I do have another child in the near future, then we may have to think about moving to a different space in the restaurant.

I shiver with anticipation. The thought of being here next year with a sweet newborn as well as my adorable daughter makes me feel so happy. I cross my fingers, my mind wandering into a daydream of two little ones playing together and then both cuddling up to me for a bedtime story. I'm lost in my thoughts, the swirl of aimable chatter is flowing around me until, suddenly, a hush descends over our group.

I look around and see that Alicia, unbeknownst to her, has chosen to sit in Patrick's designated spot. I wonder what my father-in-law's reaction is going to be. I fold my arms, watching the scene through slitted eyes.

'Alicia,' Jack says gently. 'That's Dad's seat.'

Alicia's mouth makes an 'O' shape. 'It's... it's your dad's seat?' she stutters and I can almost see the cogs of her mind whirring as she tries to fathom how a seat in a fancy restaurant could belong to her new father-in-law.

'Yes,' Jack explains patiently. 'You see, we come here every Christmas and we all tend to—'

'Oh Jack, don't be so silly. Alicia can sit there. It's about time Patrick had a change,' Dawn says.

Patrick is looking stony-faced about this, which makes it obvious that he doesn't agree with Dawn at all. I know why Patrick likes that seat. It's because he has the view out the window but he's also just at the side of the partition wall. This means he can peer out to see if there's any of his acquaintances in the main area of the restaurant and he can also easily catch the eye of passing waitresses.

Alicia jumps up. 'So sorry, I didn't realise.' A tell-tale blush of embarrassment has crept up her neck. This seems to be a common theme with her: she has a spectacular knack of managing to inadvertently put her foot in it in pretty much any social situation.

'Thank you, my dear,' Patrick says, quickly claiming the seat Alicia has just vacated.

'Oh really, Patrick, what difference does it make.' Dawn sighs.

'It's okay,' Alicia says graciously. 'I completely relate to having a favourite seat. I'm exactly the same with the cuddle chair in our flat.'

I think Alicia has recovered from this faux-pas pretty admirably – definitely an improvement on things so far.

Dawn chuckles. 'They are such comfy little seats,' she agrees, adding, 'See, you do have something in common with your new daughter-in-law after all.'

Ouch. Dawn rarely thinks about what she's saying; she has absolutely no filter. I'm used to her ways, so it's unlikely she meant anything by this statement. But Alicia, of course, looks shocked. And I don't blame her, because it sounds like they've been discussing her in an unfavourable way.

I observe Alicia, who is now fiddling with her cutlery. She's wearing a figure-hugging silver dress and she looks beautiful. But she's not cut out to be part of this family. I wonder how long she's going to last?

She might not even make it to the end of this holiday...

Chapter Nine

Alicia

Never in my life have I dined somewhere as posh as this. In the few short months since we've been married, Jack has taken me to some snazzy places in London. But this is on a whole different level. I have no idea how much money Patrick Silver has to his name, but it's more than I first imagined. For me, a girl who grew up in an average family, it feels so weird to be rubbing shoulders with such wealth, let alone being part of it.

As we make our way through the restaurant, towards the special area that has been booked out for us, I almost have to pinch myself. As a teenager, seeing the struggles my working-class parents went through, I swore to myself that I would build a future that didn't involve scrimping at the end of every month. It was my parents' dream that I would make something of myself and, since losing them both one year apart, my drive to make a successful life for myself has shaped my day-to-day living. And now I'm here, I've finally made it.

The restaurant has been tastefully decorated for the festive season. There's so much to look at, including an expansive fireplace complete with a roaring fire, a magnificent Christmas tree at the centre of the room, tables brimming with happy families talking and laughing, and an incredible ornate plaster ceiling with a stunning chandelier. Piano music is tinkling in the background and the atmosphere is jolly in the brightly lit room.

The waiter in his smart black uniform shows us to our table, where Yasmin and Ronan are already seated. Even though the sky is an inky black, there's an exceptional view of the Wicklow mountains out of the window, the full moon and stars highlighting the landscape just beyond the restaurant. I'm starting to understand why the Silver family raves about this place so much. I'm sure this will quickly become my favourite night out too. Patrick has moved on from his complaints about the taxi ride now and spirits seem high. The table is beautifully decorated, with ornate Christmas crackers, pretty candles and a festive themed tablecloth.

Zara takes a seat and so I follow suit, choosing one of the chairs nearest to the partition wall.

The talking stops and everyone goes quiet. I look around me, trying to work out what happened to cause the sudden silence.

'Alicia,' Jack says gently. 'That's Dad's seat.'

My mouth makes an 'O' shape. 'It's... it's your dad's seat?' I stutter as I process his meaning. We're in a fancy restaurant, surely Patrick hasn't paid to reserve this seat for him and him only?

'Yes,' Jack explains patiently. 'You see, we come here every Christmas and we all tend to—'

The reasons why my father-in-law has a designated seat at The Mount seem to come at me from all directions, as Dawn begins to talk over Jack. I want to rewind the clock again as it seems I've made another error in judgement. I look up to see a stony expression on my father-in-law's face. It's clear that he wants me to move. I immediately jump out of the seat.

'So sorry, I didn't realise.' A blush of embarrassment creeps up my neck. How do I manage to keep making so many missteps?

'Thank you, my dear,' Patrick says, quickly claiming the revered seat.

'Oh really, Patrick, what difference does it make,' Dawn chides him.

I want to smooth this over so I garble something about having a favourite seat at home.

Dawn chuckles and I exhale. Hopefully, this will be forgotten about quickly, by all of us.

But then Dawn nudges Patrick and says, 'See, you do have something in common with your new daughter-in-law after all.'

What did she just say? I can't keep the shocked expression from my face.

Dawn picks up the menu, oblivious to my hurt feelings, and starts to muse over the selection of delicious options on offer. I can't believe she just said that. It was such a cutting remark – and so unnecessary. I'm sure that Patrick and Dawn have talked about me between themselves, both my character and my suitability as a wife for Jack, but she didn't need to reveal that to everyone. It's also true that I probably don't have much in common with Patrick Silver, but did she really need to emphasise that as well?

I stare down at the cutlery, feeling hot and clammy. I try not to let the remark get to me. I need to make it my mission to find some common ground with Patrick and I need to do a better job of understanding Dawn. Neither of them are going to be easy people to win over.

'Oooh, I think I might have the colcannon soup to start with.' Dawn is practically licking her lips at the prospect of the food on offer. 'What are you going to have, sweetie?' she asks Zara.

'A salad,' Zara mumbles, still not willing to be cajoled into enjoying the festivities.

Having seen the interactions between Dawn and Patrick this evening, I wonder what Dawn's background is. She has a prominent Essex accent, but, other than that, I don't know much about her at all. How did she meet Patrick? Does she have money to her name as well? What happened to Zara's father? There are quite a few things I'd like to find out about my stepmother-in-law and perhaps doing a little digging about who she is and what makes her tick will help me to find a way to build a friendship with her.

It strikes me that if Dawn isn't from as affluent a background as Patrick and his sons this could be a good bonding point between the two of us. I also might be able to learn a thing or two from her about being a wife to a Silver man, as well as discovering more about Patrick through her. My brain spins with possibilities and I feel buoyed by my ideas to learn more about this family and ensure that I become a key member.

Although I'm a fish out of water in the Silvers' world right now, I'm a fast learner. I may not be the loudest voice in the room but that's okay because I understand who I am and what I want. Jack was very much part of my plan for the life I strived for. I wasn't really aware of his family connections or the money he came from to begin with, but, I have to say, that's been a very nice bonus to my husband's package.

I scan the menu – there's so much choice that I hardly know where to start.

'What are you having?' I whisper to Jack.

'Definitely the lamb cobbler. It's one of the best dishes they do, in my opinion.'

'Really, perhaps I'll have to try to steal the recipe then.'

'I'm sure they keep it under lock and key,' Jack replies. 'It will be a hard piece of information to get hold of.'

'Challenge accepted,' I say playfully, hooking my foot around his leg under the table. 'Anything for my husband.'

Jack is grinning at me like the cat who got the cream. I'm loving this newly-wed bubble.

Truth be told, I'm not entirely sure what half of the things on the menu are, so I make a mental note to google some of the dishes so I know what's what before our next visit. The amount of cutlery in front of me is also cause for concern. Looking at all the different silverware lined up, each with a different purpose that's unbeknownst to me, I recall the movie *Titanic* and the scene where Leonardo DiCaprio is similarly confused by the upper-class dining etiquettes. I cast my mind back and remember something about using the cutlery on the outside first. I'm sure that was it. But I will be keeping a beady eye on what everyone else is doing; I don't want to make another slip-up like I did when I sat in Patrick's seat.

'You must come over to visit this summer,' Patrick is telling Jack. 'The golf course here is one of the best. Ronan and I played a few times this year, you missed out.'

'It would be good to stay in the summer,' Jack agrees. 'I've not spent a summer in Ireland for years.'

'Exactly. About time you made a bit more effort with your family.'

I feel Jack flinch beside me. To say Patrick is plainly spoken is putting it mildly. He's to the point and doesn't mince his words.

'Yes, do come over in the summer,' Dawn follows up, looking at me. 'The spa here is out of this world. So relaxing.'

'I can vouch for that,' Yasmin chips in. 'If we don't get snowed in, why don't we make a day of it before New Year? I could do with a decent massage.'

Dawn's reaction to this is excitable to say the least. 'Why didn't I think of that! What a marvellous idea! Zara, sweetie, I don't think you've made it to the spa yet. It will do you good.'

Zara says nothing, her head still in the menu. Maybe she is trying to work out what everything is as well. A spa day sounds heavenly, though and just the idea of it lifts my spirits. I hope we don't get snowed in so it's possible.

'Let's do our Christmas crackers!' Dawn suggests.

Yasmin peers cautiously into Lily's pram but the baby still seems to be sleeping. 'Not too loud though,' Yasmin says in a low voice. 'I don't want Lily to wake up before the food arrives.'

'Oh, nonsense!' Dawn protests. 'You need to be noisy around babies so they get used to it. Otherwise you'll be forever tiptoeing around them. You'll have it tough when she gets to the terrible twos if you've mollycoddled her too much.'

I detect a glimmer of annoyance on Yasmin's face at this remark.

'She's right, you know,' Patrick says, nodding his head.

I find it hard to imagine Patrick as a young father, running round after two small boys, but I guess he must have got his parenting experience when Jack and Ronan were younger. Jack doesn't say much about his childhood. The most I've gleaned from him are fond memories with his grandmother in Ireland. He never mentions his mum much, but he's talked to me about her a few times, usually when he's overtired and saturated with wine. He took her passing hard and it sounds like they were close. It's something we have a mutual understanding of, losing the person who gave you life just as you're finding your way in the world.

Dawn waggles her shiny blue Christmas cracker. 'Let's do this!' She goes to pull hers with Patrick.

'Wait!' I say. 'Let's pull them all together, in a circle, like this.' I demonstrate crossing my arms over with my cracker in one hand and Jack's in the other.

'What a nice touch,' Dawn comments.

I smile. 'This was one of my parents' festive traditions. Because there were three of us, it meant we could pull our crackers together.'

'That's sweet,' Jack beams, looking around the table. Everyone is poised and ready to go.

'One. Two. Three!'

There's lots of popping from the crackers and surprised noises from the adults. I also yelp. Pulling a cracker is one of those things you're prepared for but either the sound or the movement still manages to make you jump.

'Oh no, I've dropped mine on the floor!' Ronan disappears under the table to retrieve the contents of his cracker.

'Perfect, the colour of this lipstick is gorgeous!' Dawn exclaims, holding her prize aloft. 'These are quality crackers, these are. Not like the tat we used to get, eh Zara?'

Zara looks aghast. She stretches her hand out and points across the table. 'Alicia!' she yells.

I'm startled by the volume of her voice, but, at the same time, I realise why Zara is shouting at me.

'Your dress!'

'Oh my goodness!' I jolt up from my seat. 'Jack! Help me!'

To my horror, I realise the wide sleeve of my silvery dress is alight. I'm on fire.

'Crikey!' Patrick shouts. Jack swears.

The yellow flames are dancing along the long, wide sleeve by my wrist and starting to work their way upwards, the bottom of my left arm instantly feels scorching hot.

'Move!' Yasmin shoves my husband out of the way and, before I can protest, I feel ice-cold water hit me. Yasmin has thrown the entire contents of a jug of water at me.

I reel backwards from the shock of the cold liquid. I'm drenched. The water hit me in my chest area, splattering droplets up onto my face that I know will cause my make-up to run, and cascading all down the front of me. My burning sleeve got a few splashes of liquid but not enough to defuse the situation.

'Waiter!' I hear my husband call.

Did Yasmin deliberately miss? The thought flashes into my mind and quickly fizzles away. I've got a more pressing situation to think about. But, just as I'm reaching for my own tall glass of water, a force knocks me over and I tumble to the floor.

'Down! Stifle the oxygen! That's it!'

I find my arm being pressed to the ground and Patrick is on the floor with me, trying to fan out the sparks of fire with a menu. But he just makes it worse and I yelp in pain as the flames hit my skin.

There's lots of movement going on around me and, very quickly, a waiter comes to my rescue dousing my burning sleeve with water before patting my arm down with a fire-resistant blanket. The heat cools and I sigh with relief.

'Alicia, Alicia, are you hurt?' Jack is sitting beside me on the floor and gently manoeuvres me to an upright position. 'Let me look at your arm.'

The waiter who put out the flames intervenes and introduces one of his colleagues, who's apparently trained in first aid. I'm advised not to pull at the sleeve in case the material has melted to my skin.

'Come with me,' the kindly waitress ushers me away from the table and into a little room nearby and Jack follows in our wake.

'Oh my...' I shake my head, tears spilling down my cheeks. 'I can't believe that just happened!'

'Never mind that, let's get your arm looked at,' Jack says, his face a picture of concern.

The waitress carefully cuts through the sleeve of the sequinned dress. The material has not melted onto my skin so she gently assesses the damage. Thankfully, it's not as bad as it looks. The sleeve of the dress is ruined and I have a mild burn along my wrist. But that's nothing compared to the way my ribs are aching from Patrick bundling me to the floor.

'You're very lucky,' the waitress tells me.

I don't feel lucky at all right now. The opposite: I feel extremely unlucky.

'That could have been really nasty.' She cleans up the mess and bandages up my wrist. 'Do you want some painkillers?'

I wince. 'No, but I'll have a large glass of something strong.'

'Sit here for as long as you need to.' The waitress gets me to sign an accident report with my good hand and then disappears to fulfil my drinks request.

'That was so... so...' Jack struggles to finish his sentence.

'Clumsy?' I supply. I wrinkle my nose, the faint smell of burning still filing my nostrils.

Jack kisses me on the forehead and then gives me a hug.

I sigh deeply. 'Urgh, I'm doing everything wrong today.'

'Look, it's been a long day. The main thing is that you're not too badly hurt.'

I let him hold me. Although my wrist stings, it's my pride that's really damaged.

After a few more minutes, we rejoin our table. The area has been straightened out and it looks as though nothing has happened. Everyone fusses around me and Jack thanks Yasmin and Patrick for their attempts to help. I hear Patrick say to Dawn that he will be giving the hero waiter a big tip as a thank you for his quick actions.

I try to behave as though it wasn't a big deal, even though I'm still shaking.

As everyone else is talking, I look at the layout of the table and the spot where the candle, which has now been removed, was positioned. It's so odd. I can't work out how on earth I managed to catch my sleeve alight.

I look up and I see Yasmin watching me intently. And then I remember her poorly aimed throw – I still feel damp on the front of my dress. But that doesn't bother me half as much as the renewed niggle that my sister-in-law deliberately wasted the water and threw the contents of the jug at my torso rather than over my sleeve.

She is sitting at a spaced distance from me, but there's no one in between us, just an empty chair. Is it possible that she moved the candle so that it was in my way?

Was she trying to injure me on purpose?

Chapter Ten

Yasmin

A waitress comes along to take our orders. It's perfect timing and a good distraction from the spectacle that Alicia has just caused.

'A pint of the black stuff,' Patrick declares and Ronan follows suit. I'm not a fan of Guiness but it's the drink of choice for the Silver men.

Alicia has already finished one glass and orders another Jack Daniel's and Coke. I notice that her hand is trembling a little, she must be shaken up after what just happened. I saw the flame of the candle as it connected with the material of Alicia's dress. It was her fault for being so unobservant and now the whole family is fawning round her, even though she's got little more than a slight burn.

'A white wine spritzer for me,' I say, a hint of impatience in my voice. 'With soda.'

'Do you think you should be having that?' Ronan asks me, without even attempting to whisper.

'It's Christmas, leave the lass alone!' Patrick interjects.

The waitress hurries away with our orders, extracting herself from a family debate.

'You're not still breastfeeding are you?' Dawn enquires nosily, turning her attention away from Alicia.

'No...'

'You're pregnant! I knew it!' Dawn has thrown her arms in the air and then she's out of her chair and hugging me.

'Um, it's not definite,' I try to say, glaring at Ronan over Dawn's shoulder.

'That's grand, son, good on you.' Patrick is slapping Ronan on the back and shaking his hand.

'Wait!' I say, my voice high-pitched, I'm aware this is getting out of control quickly. 'It's not certain yet, I haven't done a test.'

'The second I saw you I thought you might be pregnant again,' Dawn beams, as if I'm months along and clearly showing.

'I'm a couple of weeks late in my cycle, that's all. Let's not get ahead of ourselves.'

'I can feel it in my bones,' Dawn insists, sitting back down.

Our round of drinks is delivered efficiently.

'It's time for a toast!' Patrick announces happily. 'To the Silver family!'

We all raise our full glasses.

'To Alicia and Lily, the latest additions to our brood,' Patrick adds. 'And to another grandchild in the not-too-distant future!'

He tips his glass towards me and I clink mine with his, all the while feeling furious with Ronan for letting this conversation spiral. I give my husband a sharp kick under the table to let him know I'm not happy.

'Slainte!' Ronan cries and the rest of the family repeat the familiar Irish phrase.

Out of the corner of my eye, I notice Jack giving me a dark look. It catches me off guard. Jack and I usually get on well. So I'm not sure what his problem is. Perhaps he didn't like the news of our potential new baby overshadowing the toast to his new wife. I've found that Ronan and Jack can be very competitive, especially over sports but also in their personal and professional achievements as well. I guess that's siblings for you.

Lily begins to yowl in her pram. I'm not surprised with all the noise going on around her. I pick her up and hold her close, patting her back and rocking her, but she's restless and kicking her little legs. I'm sure she must be teething as she's been so unsettled lately. I turn her around so she can see her family seated at the table, hoping this might distract her from her grizzling. It works! Lily begins to babble, trying to talk but not quite there with forming the words yet. Everyone's smiling at her, even Zara – what an icebreaker kids can be.

We order our food and I start to relax, passing Lily over to Dawn, who's busy clucking and fussing over her.

Just as the food is delivered to our table, I see Lily's face turn red as she screws up her face. And then I catch a whiff of something. Great timing. I knew the moment of calm wouldn't last and I was right.

'Yasmin, here you go,' Dawn says, passing her over. 'Lily needs a nappy change.' Once my daughter is back in my arms, Dawn turns to Patrick and says, 'That's the beauty of grandchildren, you can hand them back and you don't have to change their nappies!'

She chortles away at this, giving no thought to how I might feel about this remark. 'I've done my time!' Dawn adds, looking pointedly at Zara, who arches an eyebrow.

'Right, I'll be back as quick as I can then,' I say to no one in particular. It would be nice if, once in a while, Ronan would just roll his sleeves up and take over, but my husband has got away with very few nappy changes in the last eleven months. He pitched in to begin with, in the first two weeks when we were both at home and I was still recovering from the birth. But once he went back to work, nappy changes have pretty much all been covered by me unless I nag him, which, quite frankly, is more exhausting than the nappy change itself.

I find the baby changing room and I manage to wipe, moisturise and change at lightning speed. All the while, I'm feeling resentful of my husband. I need to start making some changes in our relationship dynamic and his role as a father, especially if we do have another baby on the way.

He's always quick to point out that he's busy at work and that's why he can't be as hands on as he'd like. But he forgets that I work alongside him and I know exactly how many work-related tasks he has to do of a day. I may only be officially working two days a week currently, but my workload isn't massively different to his across the week. I cram as much productivity as I can in to those two days, whereas Ronan leisurely spins things out across five days and also goes for long, gossipy work lunches with clients. When I first went back to work, my husband suggested that we get a full-time nanny to help out, especially at night-time. I was briefly tempted, but I just felt it wasn't the right decision for me. I wanted to soak up the time I had with Lily, no matter how tiring that might be with juggling a demanding job as well. I managed to get a two-day slot with a nanny share in Dublin. The nanny, Orla, came highly recommended by close friends and her availability to take on new children was rare. So I snapped her up while I could. Orla is at our house one day a week with Lily and two-year-old Ben. The little boy is the child of one of my best friends, Aoife, who lives nearby us in Dublin. On the other day, Lily is at Aoife's house with Ben. It works well as it means Lily has a day playing in familiar surroundings and another day in a different environment to stimulate her.

I pick Lily up and give her a kiss on the nose. She rewards me by saying, 'Mama'. I laugh. Lily is adorable, her blonde hair tied into two little pigtails, with a couple of flyaway curls escaping the bows. I hug her tightly.

As I rejoin the group, I'm pleased to see a high chair has been added and I pop Lily down in her seat. It's far too late for her to be awake and this is going to throw her carefully planned routine off completely, but it's worth it for the mouth-watering food they serve here.

'Mmm, this is delicious!' Dawn can always be relied on to be theatrical. And when one of the waiters comes to check if we're happy with the meals, she spends a good few minutes waxing lyrical about how divine her stout-braised steak is. The staff seem pleased by her compliments. I'm sure they're looking forward to a nice, big tip later on.

Lily sits and chews some mash potato and broccoli, immediately staining her cute pink dress with green streaks. It keeps her entertained though, and I'm able to eat a hot meal for a change.

As I'm savouring my divine food, I can't help but notice the snow is continuing to fall on the Wicklow mountains and I'm sure it's getting heavier with every passing minute. I elbow Ronan. 'The weather is getting worse.'

He grunts in response, not easily distracted from the lamb cobbler he's wolfing down. Everyone else also has their eyes down, enjoying their expensive food.

After finishing my meal, I make my excuses and head to the ladies' to freshen up. On my way there, I find the restaurant has emptied out a lot. There are only a couple of tables left now, the pianist is playing to just a handful of people. The majority of these diners look as though they are winding up their evenings and one group of people are shrugging on their coats. I check my watch, it's 9.30 p.m. and usually this place is buzzing until gone midnight.

'Are you okay there?' a young waiter asks me, his hair slicked back and his uniform pristine.

'Are guests leaving early due to the weather?' I blurt out my concern.

'Yes, a number of our diners have a fair journey home and they didn't want to get caught out in the snowstorm tonight.'

'What's the forecast looking like for the next few hours?'

'The snow is predicted to get even heavier later on, but it seems to have started up earlier than expected.'

I thank the waiter and then escape to the loos. My mind is made up: I want to get Lily back to Bartley Lodge as soon as possible. Patrick isn't going to like it, but I'm not going to risk getting stuck in the snow with a baby in the taxi.

'Ronan, can I have a word.' Back at the table, I crook my finger to indicate I want to speak with my other half privately. He gets up, looking happy after his hearty meal. 'We need to go. The weather is set to get worse and the restaurant has emptied out.'

Ronan looks around and sees what I mean.

'I know Patrick won't be best pleased, but I want to get Lily back before the roads get too blocked.'

'You're right,' Ronan agrees quickly. 'We need to get you both back, especially in your condition.'

'Ronan, you promised not to get carried away,' I scold him.

'Sorry, sweetheart, I'm just excited.' He kisses me on the cheek and flings an arm around my shoulder. He's a few Guinness's down now and merry with it.

We return to the table. Ronan doesn't say anything, so I realise he's going to leave it to me to tell his father that we're going. 'Patrick, I'm sorry, but we're going to make our way back now. The weather is getting bad and I want to get Lily safely tucked up in her cot before it's too late.'

'What about your Porter cake?' Dawn asks, dismay written across her face.

'Surely it's not that awful, it's only a bit of the white stuff!' Patrick grumbles, before taking a long sip of his Guinness.

Ronan replies, 'It's not easing up, though, you know how the weather can turn up here. I want to get Yasmin back, we don't want to get stuck on a hill somewhere.'

'We may as well all go then,' Dawn says. 'I'll ask the staff if they can box up the desserts so we can take them home with us. We can eat them with a nice Irish coffee when we get back.' Dawn places a hand on Patrick's arm to placate him and he doesn't protest about leaving any further.

Ronan pulls his phone out of his pocket and goes through the motions of organising the cabs to come as soon as possible.

I'm relieved that we're heading back without too much fuss.

But I'm not looking forward to being trapped in the same house as Alicia during the snowstorm.

Chapter Eleven

Jack

The evening out hasn't gone too well. In fact, it's been a total disaster. Alicia has been nervous and jittery for the entirety of the last few hours. I've tried to put her at ease, but she somehow keeps slipping up. More than that, she's a complete wreck. She is usually fairly self-contained. Sure, she's prone to anxious thoughts but is generally collected and together on the outside. She's never been the life and soul of the party but she tends to get on with most people in her own amiable way. In private, she relaxes more and I get to witness the cheekier side of her personality. But tonight it's like her nerves have got the better of her, and the accident with the candle only made things worse.

Seeing Alicia's sleeve catching fire from the candle flame sent shockwaves through me. But I'm useless in emergency situations and the best I could do was call a member of staff over. Although, thank God I did as things could have taken a nasty turn if they'd been left unchecked for much longer.

Now we're all gulping down our drinks and being handed our desserts in flimsy cardboard boxes. The evening didn't really get started and has been abruptly curtailed. If only we'd had a bit longer here, the mood might have brightened up. Returning to the lodge is the right call, given the situation with the weather, but I can't help but think the car ride back is going to be just as painful as the drive to the restaurant. If only we'd all had the chance to have a couple more drinks, as it might have loosened everyone up. Instead, the atmosphere now is even more strained than it was at the start of the meal.

We wait twenty minutes until one black cab eventually turns up. It's the one with a child's seat in, so Ronan, Yasmin and Lily are spirited off into the darkness. The rest of us sit in the lounge area of the restaurant, in comfortable velvet-upholstered chairs around the roaring fire. Alicia has selected the furthest chair away from the hearth, and I don't blame her after what happened. But I'm enjoying the warmth that's relaxing my tense muscles, along with the pleasant after-effects of my last drink of whiskey.

'Another round,' my father barks at a passing waiter. The grandfather clock nearby is ticking loudly, marking every passing minute and my father is once again becoming agitated. 'I bet it's the eejit that dropped us here,' he moans about the taxi driver, whilst conveniently forgetting the same man suggest arranging an earlier pick up.

Another ten minutes stretch on, I look over at my wife and note that her pretty dress is ruined and her eyes are downcast. Maybe this holiday was a bad idea. Alicia hasn't been exposed to my family for any significant amount of time and this is probably going to be an overwhelming week for her. In hindsight, we should've had our first Christmas together as a married couple on our own. We've got years ahead of us for big family holidays.

Except I wanted us to be here on this festive trip. It's important to me that Alicia bonds with my family and that she gets to know them properly as fast as she can. It's all part of my plan. Part of the reason why I married Alicia so quickly.

I realise I haven't given my wife much guidance or context to help her get to know the various members of my family. She's been thrown in at the deep end, so I need to rectify this. I start thinking about the little snippets of information I could give her, tips for conversation starters, things to avoid saying or doing. I should have thought about all of this before we arrived in Ireland. I assumed she'd be a natural and would easily fit in on this Christmas holiday. But if my plan is going to work, it's clear I need to zoom in on the finer details and give Alicia some tips to help her navigate the different personalities she's encountering.

I'm lost in thought, my eyes fixed on the bright flames in front of me, when a member of staff strides over to let us know that our cab has finally arrived. We all bundle outside and find our places in the taxi.

'Hello again.' It's a familiar voice, the voice of the driver who took us to The Mount.

I cross my fingers, hoping the man has the sense to keep his thoughts to himself. The last thing we need is for my father to be antagonised on the trip home. The evening has been awful enough as it is.

'I thought I'd be seeing you again before eleven p.m.,' the driver says with a hint of glee in his voice. He knows he's got one over on the pompous man sitting on the back seat of his cab, but why can't he just take quiet satisfaction in this? Surely he doesn't want to piss off a wealthy client?

'Thanks for coming to get us,' I reply smoothly, taking control of the situation. 'We'd appreciate it if you could get us back safely and speedily. My wife has had a bit of an ordeal tonight and we're keen to get home.'

I made sure I was as courteous possible. My words were chosen to be polite to the man who's about to steer us along treacherous, icy roads and also to save face for my father. I've used Alicia's incident as the reason for us leaving early and hopefully this will serve to extinguish the macho pride on both sides of the glass partition in the taxicab.

My father gives me a short nod and I'm relieved that he appreciated my intervention.

'Righto,' says the driver. 'Say no more.'

With that, the glass between the passenger seats and the driver's section slides over and the vehicle pulls away from The Mount. As I glance back over my shoulder, I notice that the twinkling lights around the entrance to the restaurant are flickering ominously. There must be something wrong with the connection, but the effect makes me shudder. I'm not usually superstitious, but there's something about the blinking lights that turns my stomach.

The driver has got his work cut out driving up the sloping roads towards our holiday lodge. We could probably have booked out rooms at the hotel attached to The Mount, but, if we're about to get snowed in for the next few days, it's best we're at the lodge where we have home comforts and plenty of supplies.

I give Alicia a warm smile. I feel anything but confident about the drive back, but I want to reassure my wife as much as possible. Dawn's chatter fills the car, distracting us all from the bumpy ride. Dawn talks about the coming days, making plans for entertaining ourselves in the countdown to Christmas. Zara chips in a little bit; she seems rejuvenated after the excellent food and drink.

My stepsister can be moody and reserved, but I've also seen her in happier states of mind. Those times are usually when she's not with

Dawn and the rest of the family. Zara is a freelance designer and, every so often, we meet up in London for a pint or two. It's not a frequent thing, but she's cool to hang out with outside of the family enclosure. Like Alicia, Zara appears quiet and reserved, but there's a lot more to her when you scratch the surface.

The taxi jerks its way up the snowy incline, but, despite the less than smooth course of the journey, I'm impressed the driver is managing to keep the vehicle moving even if we're going at a snail's pace. The time seems to drag on, but at least we're continuing to move forward. And then, suddenly, the car swerves, losing its grip and slips along the icy track. I hold my breath and Alicia gives a little yelp of concern. I have visions of us continuing to slide downwards, all the way back along the hilly road we've just inched along. Or worse, the car tumbling sideways, flipping over and over down the mountainside.

The car skids to a halt.

'Sorry about that!' the driver calls.

We all exhale. At least we've stopped, but what now?

'I'm going to need you all to jump out for a minute,' the driver says, sliding back the hatch to speak to us.

'Whatever for?' my father demands.

'I need to push the cab back onto the road, we hit some black ice and swerved off course.'

'No worries, I'll help,' I volunteer, once again intervening between the butting heads of the two older men.

Everyone climbs out slowly. It's freezing cold. I'm concerned by the thought of the cab breaking down in the sub-zero temperature and us all having to wait for hours for help. So I zip up my coat and go and help the driver. We work together to heave and shove the vehicle back onto the main road. Zara mucks in too, while the others stay back, huddling close for warmth, and watching as we strain and push the black cab out of the snowy bank. It takes an enormous effort, but we manage to get the vehicle back on the road.

We all climb back into our seats and the driver gets us moving again. We're going even slower this time and the rest of the journey is incredibly nail-biting. I take Alicia's left hand and hold it between mine Staring out of the window, I look for familiar landmarks, but everything is covered in a blanket of white. After what feels like hours, we climb towards the gravel driveway that leads to our holiday lodge and the driver pulls over.

'There you go, folks, I'm not going to attempt that last incline so I'll drop you here.'

'Thanks very much,' I respond swiftly. I slide a few notes over to the driver, by way of a tip. 'Will you be all right getting back?' I ask.

The driver looks at me, surprised. I'm hoping he won't want to take up a room for the night, but, in the circumstances, I have to ask. I don't want him to have an accident on the way back and for that to be on my conscience.

'Yeah, pal, I'll be grand.'

I shake his hand and then follow the others out of the cab and up the snow-covered path before turning to watch the vehicle slip and slide its way into the dark night.

I watch my breath, visible in front of me in the frosty air.

We made it back in one piece.

We made it back alive.

Chapter Twelve

Now

The handcuffs bite into my wrists as I'm half lifted, half dragged between two burly Garda officers. My teeth are chattering from the cold and the fear welling up inside me.

I'm vaguely aware of one of the officers reading me my rights, and it feels so surreal. Words from TV programmes and films floating in the chill air. 'You do not have to say anything...'

I couldn't say anything even if I tried. The shock at finding the dead body and then being immediately arrested, accused of murder, has resulted in my brain freezing, unable to respond to what's going on around me.

I let my body go limp and allow myself to be spirited across the snow with no resistance. Bartley Lodge is now in sight, light emitting from the windows and reminding me that, just a few hours ago, everything was normal. Now nothing will ever be the same again.

One of the officers shoulders open the front door and shoves me inside.

I stumble and trip, flat on my face, my arms bound behind me and unable to break my fall. A pain sears in my cheekbone and tears sting in my eyes. I want to cry out, but I've lost all control of my voice.

An officer hauls me back to my feet.

I blink rapidly to clear my eyes and when my vision unmists, I see four shocked faces staring at me from the other end of the hallway.

'What's going on?' a voice cries.

If only I could explain...

Chapter Thirteen

Alicia

I turn over, my eyes fluttering open as the morning light filters through a gap in the curtain. I feel warm and cosy, the thick duvet half wrapped around me, and I sigh as I'm greeted by the face of my gorgeous husband.

'Morning,' I say, scootching closer to him.

Jack yawns widely and murmurs something under his breath.

'What was that?' I ask him softly.

'You stole all the covers,' he groans.

I look over at him, half in and half out of the duvet and see that he's right. We never seem to get the duvet sharing right, one of us always ends up out in the cold. I puff up the duvet cover and throw more of the bedcovers over him. Jack settles back onto the pillow and, almost immediately, he is snoring once again.

I lay still for a minute, trying to work out why I have an odd sensation swirling inside me. I have a strong feeling of something being awry. Then it all comes rushing back to me: last night, the candle, the burn, the water, the hair-raising journey back to the lodge.

I gingerly lift up my left arm and gently prod the bandage just below my wrist. My skin feels tight and uncomfortable underneath it. But, more than that, my ego is also bruised. There's no way I want to get up yet and face Jack's family once more.

I settle back down, tossing and turning for a bit, trying to get comfortable. I'm just drifting off again when there's a sharp knock at the door.

'Wakey, wakey,' comes a sing-song voice. And then Dawn barges open our bedroom door and is in the room, standing at the foot of our double bed.

Jack sits up abruptly, rudely awoken from his slumber, while I half-squeal and pull the duvet up over my chin.

'Dawn!' my husband exclaims croakily.

'Rise and shine, you two!' Dawn is dressed in another fluffy jumper, a powder-blue one today, her hair blow-dried to perfection and her face fully made up. 'Breakfast is ready,' she continues, unaware of her intrusion. 'And Patrick wants to get out for a family walk now it's stopped snowing.'

Neither Jack or I move or say a word in response.

'Chop, chop!'

'Okay, Dawn, we get the message. I'm butt naked under here, so give us some privacy, will you!'

Dawn fluffs her hair, saying, 'Don't be too long!'

'Sorry about that,' Jack mutters when she's finally left.

'She's pretty full on, isn't she?'

'That's one way of putting it!'

'I can smell pancakes!' Jack exclaims, leaping out of bed and scurrying into the en-suite.

I don't know how he does that. He goes from being in a deep sleep to wide awake and ready to face the day in the space of a few seconds.

I'm the kind of person who usually needs to set my alarm clock at least five times, so I can hit snooze for the first few buzzers and slowly uncurl myself from my sleepy state. Although Dawn's unwelcome entrance into our bedroom has certainly shocked me into being wide awake this morning.

I hear the shower go on and decide to stay where I am for five minutes longer. I can just about hear voices downstairs, but I can't make out who they belong to. Jack's right, the smell of pancakes is wafting up to our room. And they smell glorious.

Jack is soon out of the shower and starts to pull his trousers on. So I get up and make my way into the bathroom, brushing my teeth and splashing my face with water as my first rituals of the day. I get ready hurriedly, throwing on skinny jeans and a festive jumper. Together, Jack and I make our way downstairs.

'Morning,' Dawn beams. She seems to be in a jolly mood this morning. 'Who wants potato and spring onion breakfast pancakes?'

Zara is standing behind Dawn with her back to me. She flips a large pancake up into the air and it spins and lands in the pan. She repeats the action again with a flick of her wrist, and once again the pancake effortlessly turns and falls back into the pan.

'Yum! Yes please,' Jack replies enthusiastically.

There's music playing on low in the background and I cock my head and listen intently, trying to work out what the song is. But then Patrick bursts into the room singing along to the tune at the top of his voice. 'Sweet Molly Malone...'

He swoops behind Dawn and wraps his thick arms around her waist, still crooning with a smile on his face. 'Ah, you can't beat that one!' Patrick says as the song comes to an end. 'And you can't beat this breakfast either.'

He takes a plate, stacked high with the delicious savoury pancakes, and sits down at the wooden table where Yasmin, Ronan and Lily are already halfway through their food.

My eyes flick to the floor-to-ceiling window and I can see the snow has really piled up overnight, but there's currently no snowflakes in the air and the blue sky is still and bright.

Patrick takes a bite of his breakfast and makes an appreciative noise. 'The man who has luck in the morning has luck in the afternoon,' he declares.

I look at Jack, eyebrows raised questioningly.

My husband laughs. 'That might be the first time you've heard that phrase, but it sure won't be the last.'

'It definitely won't be!' Ronan chimes in. 'Dad says that line at least once a week.'

'That's because it's a good 'un and completely true as well.'

'You'll have to watch out for a few more of his catchphrases,' Jack winks at me.

And then Ronan adds, 'If you're lucky enough to be Irish... you're lucky enough!' His eyes are twinkling as he says this.

'Absolutely,' Patrick smiles.

'What are you so cheery about?' Jack enquires.

'Oh, this and that.' Patrick's reply is vague, but there's a teasing note in his voice.

'He's just closed a big business deal,' Ronan pipes up.

'One that deserves a champagne toast!' Dawn adds, brandishing a big bottle of Bollinger.

She pops the cork and it ricochets off one of the kitchen cabinets, zooming towards me and flying straight by my ear, merely an inch from my face. My heart is thumping – that was a near miss.

Dawn fills a number of glasses and hands them out. Jack and I sit down at the table and we're soon joined by Zara and Dawn.

'Slainte!' Patrick says and we all clink glasses. I have no idea what kind of deal I'm celebrating as the subject of Patrick's work has never come up between me and Jack. But now I'm curious as to what line of business my father-in-law is in. I know that he owns his own company, but beyond that, nothing. I must quiz Jack on this later.

I tuck into my potato pancakes. They're so tasty, the hint of onion is just the right balance and I enjoy the breakfast along with the fizz of champagne bubbles on my tongue.

I'm so absorbed in my food that I haven't been following the conversation properly.

'What do you think, Alicia?' Patrick asks.

My face is blank, there's no way I can fudge this. 'Sorry, what was the question?'

'Do you think it's worth risking a jaunt outside?'

I look out the window, the world looks so serene. There's no hint of the snowstorm that was raging last night. The sun is shining and the snow glistens harmlessly.

'It looks very pretty out there.' My answer doesn't commit either way, as I'm not sure who was advocating for venturing outside of the nice warm lodge. I'm not a huge fan of the cold or the outdoors generally. I can appreciate a good view, but I don't necessarily feel the need to be part of it in the way that some people do. I'm much happier indoors.

'There you go, Alicia is up for it too. Decision made.' Patrick slaps his hand down on the polished surface of the dining table.

Yasmin is pouting and looking annoyed. I join the dots and realise Yasmin was the person trying to dissuade Patrick from a wintery morning walk. Although Patrick seems like the sort of person who will do whatever he wants when his mind is made up. I doubt he would have been swayed by my thoughts or by Yasmin's.

'Babe, stay here if you'd rather,' Ronan says to Yasmin. 'You and Lil don't need to come out in the snow if you don't want to.'

'Lily will love it!' Dawn butts in. 'You can't deprive a child of the chance to run about in the snow.'

'Let's all go as a family, no one's staying indoors,' Patrick commands.

Yasmin looks even more haughty at this. Her voice silenced by Patrick's dominating presence. I'm not sure me jumping to Yasmin's defence would achieve anything, apart from upsetting my father-in-law. As it is, I've already annoyed Yasmin. And there's a part of me that still feels wary of my sister-in-law, even more so after the candle incident last night.

Yasmin runs her fingers through her dark tresses and shrugs. 'I'll come with you...' She pauses and stands up dramatically. 'But you'd better watch out because...' Yasmin smiles with a gleam in her eye.

I wait with bated breath to hear what she's going to say next.

'... You know who's going to win in a snowball fight.' Yasmin winks at Ronan and everyone laughs. The atmosphere in the room immediately feels lighter.

I look towards the other end of the long table. Zara's long hair is tied back from her face, she doesn't have any make-up on and the only piercing she has in is her nose ring.

The penny drops.

'I remember!' I say triumphantly. 'I remember where I know you from!'

Seeing Zara without her dark make-up jogs my memory. Zara and I were in the same accommodation together at university. She looks much more like the person I remember from my university days this morning. It's flooding back to me now. Zara was in the bottom-floor apartment and I was in the top-floor apartment of the same block. We weren't friends, more passing acquaintances, but she was a face I saw regularly during my first year. We'd often be at the same parties and the same gatherings. And we'd pass each other on the street on a daily basis. It all feels like such a long time ago now. I was eighteen at the time and I'm thirty-four now. It was half a lifetime ago. So no wonder I hadn't made the connection sooner, especially as Zara looks so different when she's all made up.

Zara stares at me astonished. 'I've never met you before, I told you that yesterday.'

'It was university. You were in the bottom-floor apartment, the same one as my friend Rosie, part of the East Block.'

I'm aware the other faces around the table are all looking at me and, as I finish my sentence, heads swivel in Zara's direction, waiting for her response.

She opens her mouth and then closes it again.

Before she can speak, Dawn cuts in. 'Did you go to Liverpool University?'

'Yes,' I reply.

Dawn gasps. 'So you were at the same university as Zara.'

A troubled look passes over Zara's face. She mumbles, 'I'm sorry, I just don't remember you.'

'It's okay. It was a long time ago. It's not like we spoke often, I just knew your face. That was all. Mystery solved!' My words tumble out one after the other. I'm glad I've placed Zara in my timeline and that I'm not going mad and imagining things.

Zara shrugs and picks up her coffee mug, her eyes avoiding my gaze.

'You might have friends in common, though,' Dawn persists. 'You'll have to have a good gossip about the past later on.'

Dawn starts to clear up the breakfast things. Scooping up plates and cups and dumping them in the dishwasher. I stand and help her with the task. I notice Zara move towards the kitchen door. Before she slips away, Patrick's voice booms.

'Be ready in ten minutes for our walk!'

'What a coincidence that you and Zara studied at the same place,' Dawn says, shutting the dishwasher door and switching the machine on.

'Mmm,' I respond. I feel awkward about the whole thing. Either Zara genuinely doesn't have any recollection of me or she just doesn't want to acknowledge a connection. I suspect she probably doesn't want to reminisce about her time in Liverpool and I wish I'd never said anything now.

'Zara can be a little shy.' Dawn has just popped the salt and pepper into one of the cupboards and turns to speak to me face on.

I contemplate this. Is Zara really shy? Or is she standoffish? Rude even? I can't get the measure of her.

'She'll warm up soon enough, it just takes her a bit of time.'

I nod, not sure what to say. But it's sweet that Dawn is so keen for me to get on with her daughter.

'Why don't you have a chat with her whilst we're walking? She's better one-to-one.'

'Of course.' I smile and hope this is the case. I need to form some alliances in this family. Although Dawn herself is the best ally I could have, so I'm eager to do whatever I can to get her to like me. Zara seems like the outsider, the weakest link. But she could be the key to me gaining approval from Dawn, who's clearly second-in-command after Patrick.

I need to carve out a place for myself amongst the established relationships in the Silver family. And I'm going to do whatever it takes to make myself belong in this world of wealth and luxury, with these people who have no idea how lucky they are.

Chapter Fourteen

Yasmin

What a horrid evening last night was. I couldn't get back to the lodge fast enough. The whole meal was a washout from start to finish. We should never have gone to The Mount in that weather. I'm feeling angry at being forced out into the cold, treacherous blizzard to endure an uncomfortable meal, followed by a nerve-shredding journey back to safety. I have my daughter to think of and I'm not happy about the way Patrick railroaded us all into participating in yesterday's outing.

Nor am I pleased at this being repeated this morning. I don't want to step foot outside of this lodge. It might not be snowing right now but I bet it won't be long before we start to see flurries in the air again. Patrick always takes an authoritarian attitude to decision-making when we're all together. Usually, I'm okay with this. After all, it's his holiday house so I can accept that we play by his rules. But I'm a mother now and I feel a burning resentment at being bossed about by Ronan's father. Patrick has no regard for Lily's routine, let alone any thought for what's best for his granddaughter's wellbeing. It's interesting that I'm seeing Patrick in a new light now that I'm a parent. Before Lily's arrival, I looked up to Patrick. He inspired me with his entrepreneurial spirit, but lately I've noticed more of his selfish traits.

I wipe Lily's hands and face before lifting her out of her high chair. She scrambles to get down on the floor. I watch her set off crawling, at speed, towards the open kitchen door.

In years gone by, I may have grumbled internally at Patrick's insistence on early-morning walks, however late the previous night was and despite everyone sporting hangovers. Patrick always says a long, brisk walk in the morning is the best cure for a heavy night. And, in some ways, I agree. Getting out in the fresh air often helped to shake off the after effects of alcohol. However, repeating this cycle almost every day for a week is an exhausting way to spend a holiday. So I'd often need a few days' recovery when we got back home. An opportunity to sleep in late, watch TV in my pyjamas and eat chocolate to my heart's content.

But things are different this year. I'm still up in the night with Lily at least once, sometimes twice. So there's no way I'm going to keep up with the pace of late nights and early mornings for the entirety of our stay. I'm going to have to sit out a few things, but I need to do this diplomatically. I'm still Patrick's favourite daughter-in-law and I intend for things to stay that way.

The truth is, I see Alicia as a rival. For so long, I've been the perfect wife and the perfect daughter-in-law. I don't want anyone to take that crown away from me. Least of all, a commoner like Alicia, who has no class whatsoever. I have no idea what Jack sees in her. The more time I'm spending with the new addition to the family, the less threatened I feel by her. It's obvious that she's struggling to fit in and she has no natural charm about her. But I have to make sure Alicia doesn't worm her way onto Patrick's most trusted list. Not just because it would dent my pride, there are other things in jeopardy as well...

I catch up with Lily and pluck her from the floor. I take her into the lounge, where she wriggles out of my arms and makes a beeline for the enormous Christmas tree in the corner of the room. The red, round baubles hanging from the bottom branches are in her sights. She reaches the base of the tree before I can catch up with her. Lily tugs hard at one of the shining decorations.

'Lily, no!' I cry as I rush over to her. I see the branch wobble and a handful of the natural pine needles fall in a cluster onto the wooden floor as well as covering my daughter, but, luckily, she didn't dislodge the whole tree. 'Lily, don't touch,' I say crossly. 'Leave the tree alone.'

I dust her down, making sure every last pine needle is removed from her clothing and hair. Then I pick her up once more and begin the battle of getting her into her snowsuit and wellington boots. I tell her in a clear voice that we're going to play outside. Miraculously, she doesn't fight against me putting on her outer layers.

Once my little girl is ready, I go and retrieve my own coat, hat, gloves and boots. I clasp Lily's chubby hands and help her to walk up and down the long hallway whilst we're waiting for everyone else. I have no idea where Ronan is. He promised he'd stay off his work phone during the holiday, but he keeps disappearing. I'm sure he is checking in with the staff who are working until Christmas Eve. That's the only drawback of running a business of your own, you're constantly switched on. Even on holiday. There are so many things to keep account of, so many potential pitfalls that have to be navigated. And there's always an unforeseen issue that arises as well. Whether it's someone unable to come in due to sickness or a tricky query that needs a resolution.

This year, Ronan and I have invested a lot of time in training our staff. We wanted to challenge them, stretch them and give them the tools to progress in their careers. Unfortunately, a few of them, those who would easily fit under the term 'quiet quitters', weren't up for this at all. As a result, they've moved on and it meant we had an intense round of recruitment that took up valuable time earlier in the year. The employees we have now are still newbies and they've got a way to go until they're fully fledged members of the team. It does make it harder to hand over responsibility to our employees when they're still inexperienced, even if it's only for a few days. Maybe it would have been less stressful to just shut the business while we were away, but I doubt Ronan would have agreed to that suggestion.

I just wish Ronan would learn to let go a little more. Does he really need to check in every few hours? Yes, there will always be new houses coming up for auction. Yes, there will always be new contracts that need sorting with potential tenants and maintenance that needs doing across the rental properties that we own. But these things don't need responding to immediately. A day or two's delay won't impact the big picture. My husband doesn't seem to see things like that, though. He's out to prove himself, to prove himself to be as good as his father. I'm happy to help facilitate Ronan's dream and I support him all the way. But we also need to establish a healthy work/life balance for our family, especially if we're soon to add another to our brood.

I place my hand on my stomach. I wish we could pop out and get a pregnancy test right now, so that we'd know the answer either way. There's no chance of that because of the snowfall, though, not for a good few days at least.

'Excellent!' Patrick beams at me. 'I knew you'd be ready first, Yasmin. You're always so efficient.'

I take this as a compliment and smile back at him. Lily lifts her arms out in front of her, looking imploringly at Patrick. He bends down and lifts Lily off her feet, spinning her round in a circle as my daughter giggles with glee.

'Aww, look at that!' Dawn is with us now, her phone out and snapping a picture of the cute grandfather-and-granddaughter moment. 'Just adorable!'

I feel a swell of pride at my cherub-faced child and her ability to wrap Patrick around her little finger already. It's a life skill that will serve her well in the future.

Ronan saunters in, slipping his phone into his back pocket. The unnerving thought that maybe my husband isn't checking his phone for work purposes crosses my mind. He has seemed more glued to his mobile than usual lately, but I can't let the thought torment me. I'm sure he was just touching base with the team.

Eventually, we're all ready and wrapped up. Even Nuala is coming with us. She has a thick dog coat on and is barking excitedly.

'Good girl!' Patrick opens the door and Nuala bolts outside, running around in a circle and chasing her tail.

Patrick leads the way and we all follow him and Nuala, our footprints besmirching the pristine layer of snow. I hold Lily's gloved hand in mine and she attempts to lift one foot and then the other, before realising snow is much harder to walk on. She stops and begins to wail. I look around me, hoping that my husband might step in and carry our daughter on his shoulders. But he's already striding ahead, matching his father's pace, deep in conversation.

'Come on, little one.' I smooth her hair and swing her up onto my hip. She's getting heavier by the day, but if I can catch up with everyone, then someone else might take her for a bit.

I stomp forward until I've caught up with the rest of the group. Patrick seems to be leading us towards the woodland area at the bottom of the hill. Nuala is running back and forth between everyone, barking enthusiastically and generally tearing around, releasing her pent-up energy.

Lily gurgles and claps her tiny hands, her eyes fixed on Nuala's movements. Just ahead of me, I notice Alicia reacts every time Nuala comes in her direction. The poor dog is harmless, but Alicia is wary and the canine's manic behaviour is spooking my sister-in-law. I smirk. Patrick adores Nuala – he's a dog lover, and he will hold it against Alicia if she doesn't warm to his beloved pet.

I see Ronan put his mobile phone to his ear. He looks furtively around, spots me and flashes an apologetic look. He strides off ahead, talking in a quick, low voice. I wonder what the problem is now. He should have left the phone back at the lodge.

We make our way under the canopy of trees. The snow isn't as thick on the ground here, but I look up and see many of the tree branches are weighed down heavily with white snow. I hope it's safe to be walking in these woods. I wouldn't want any of the branches above to come crashing down upon us. But I stay quiet, keeping my reservations to myself.

Ronan is back with us in minutes. 'Lily!' He waves at his daughter and she shyly waves back. 'Let me take her.' Ronan holds his arms out to Lily, but she's reluctant to leave my side at first.

'Want to go on Daddy's shoulders?'

That does the trick.

Soon, Lily is in place on my husband's shoulders. She's clutching little fistfuls of his hair and he has his hands firmly on her legs.

'Thanks,' I say. All of a sudden I feel very, very tired. I'd give anything to be back in bed right now. Perhaps I really am pregnant.

'Just look at that gorgeous smile!' Dawn turns around with her phone out in front of her as she clicks away, taking more pictures of Lily. 'See, she wouldn't have wanted to miss out on all of this.'

A rage flares inside me. I'm sick of Dawn's opinions on the way I'm raising Lily. It doesn't matter what we're doing, or how I'm doing something, she's always quick to make a snide quip, to find fault or ridicule me. I'm so fed up with it. Ronan doesn't seem to notice at all. I wonder if it's just me. Am I being paranoid?

But I don't think I am. Dawn's criticisms are too frequent to be innocent. Her desire to overrule me as a parent is something I'm subjected to every time we're together. It's more than just annoying now. She's constantly trying to put me down. And she's interfering with my choices as a mother. I wish she'd just get off my back. She never used to be like this...

I shake myself from my morose thoughts and snap back to reality.

'... It seems like a completely different life now...' Alicia is talking to Zara. They're walking a few paces in front of me, heads bent towards each other.

I'm intrigued, so I tune in properly to their conversation and listen to the two of them discussing their lives at university. And Zara reveals something very interesting indeed...

Her words get me thinking, in all the time I've known Zara she's never properly opened up to me. It seems Alicia is getting somewhere with her, though. I often think Zara is a spoilt brat. She's so self-absorbed, preoccupied with her own issues, never looking up to notice the world around her. But maybe there's another story there. One that I've missed.

This is the danger with any new addition to a family. Unless they're a little newborn, people come with history and with baggage. And there are enough problems in this family as it is, without having any more to contend with.

Chapter Fifteen
Alicia

Nuala is zipping up and down the line we're walking in. Running in a wide circle, as though she's a sheepdog rounding us up. I shiver. Nuala has long legs and sharp teeth. I've not spent much time around dogs, not even little ones so, even though I know she's a loyal family pet, my instinct is to not get too close.

'Here, girl!' Patrick calls Nuala and she runs straight to him. He bends down, fussing and patting her.

I stay at the back, away from Nuala. Patrick is walking side by side with Ronan. Jack is trailing after them, with Dawn jabbering away to him. Yasmin and Lily are a number of paces behind us. Zara and I are somewhere in the middle of the group. I didn't deliberately set out to walk with Zara, even though Dawn had encouraged me to. I'm not going to be frosty with Zara, despite her less than welcoming behaviour towards me so far. So I take a big breath and strike up a conversation.

'Just a bit cold!' I joke. With this, I bury my gloved hands as far into my coat pockets as I can. I'm wearing a thick, khaki green padded jacket that Jack bought me a few weeks ago.

'Freezing,' Zara responds. She's wearing a long leather jacket that's fleece lined and has a dark collar of black fur. Her hair is flowing over her shoulders now and her make-up and piercings are back in place. 'Patrick insists on family walks every year.'

'How long have you been coming up here at Christmastime?'

'Three years,' Zara sighs.

'That bad?' I chuckle in a low voice.

'Nah, it's fine. It's just the whole herd mentality thing that gets a bit much after a few days. I like time by myself, to read and draw.'

'I can imagine it can end up feeling a bit overwhelming after a while.'

'I've not been snowed in before, though. That's a new one.' Even in just these few passing sentences, I feel as though I'm understanding Zara's nature a bit more.

'So whereabouts are you based? Do you live with Patrick and Dawn?' I know very little about Zara, so I'm curious to hear her answer.

She shakes her head firmly. 'No!' She stops suddenly, coughing. 'Sorry,' Zara says after catching her breath. 'Just the idea of living with the two of them... No thanks!'

I laugh.

'I live on a canal boat actually.'

'Oh cool.'

'I'm a freelance designer, so I can work where I want. You can usually find me somewhere along the Grand Union Canal.'

'Nice. How long have you had the boat for?'

'Almost seven years now. I love it. It's a way of life.'

'So if you moor along the Grand Union Canal, do you ever head into London?'

'Yeah, a few times a year. I meet Jack for a beer when I'm in the city.'

This is news to me. I don't know why I find this piece of information unsettling. I guess it's because in all the years I've known Jack, I've never heard him mention Zara's name. Although I'm sure there's a lot of new things I'll learn about my husband in the coming months, in the first year of our marriage.

'Well, it would be nice to see you when you're next in town.' There's a note of stiffness in my voice, but at least I've extended the invitation.

'I don't really plan where I'm going to be, I drift along and see where life takes me, but I'll let you know when I'm next in the city.'

'That sounds like a nice, stress-free way of living.'

We fall silent for a minute or two and continue to pad through the thick snow. Patrick is leading us into a woodland area. At least it should provide some shelter from the bitter wind.

'I'm sorry if the whole university thing made you uncomfortable.' I pause and continue, 'It seems like a completely different life now...'

'It does. We're getting old!' Zara's lips are curving upwards in a half-smile, so she can't be that annoyed about me banging on about the connection.

'I can't believe you recognised me,' she continues.

'Well, I didn't at first.'

'It's all the piercings.'

'It was a long time ago, we've all changed, I'm sure.'

'I wasn't meaning to be rude. It's just... I've blocked out a lot of university. I didn't exactly have the best time there.' Zara shrugs at this.

'Oh, I'm sorry. I didn't mean to bring back bad memories.' It seems obvious now that she didn't want to recall her time at Liverpool.

''S'ok. You weren't to know.'

'No reminiscing about our early twenties, I promise. I doubt I can remember much of it now anyway, it's just a haze of too much alcohol and not enough sleep.'

Nuala comes running towards us once more and I quickly step out of her path.

'Don't you like dogs?' Zara asks.

'It's not that. I'm just not used to them.'

I look back over my shoulder, as Nuala has kept running rather than looping back round to Patrick. I realise Ronan and Yasmin are quite a way behind us, fussing over Lily. Ronan has the baby on his shoulders.

'Look, you seem all right,' Zara says, a hushed tone to her voice.

I start and turn back towards her.

'Thanks?' I'm not sure where she's going with this, but my ears prick up as I feel like it's going to be something important.

'If you want my advice, don't get too drawn in by this family.' Zara's face is serious.

'Huh?'

'I said don't get too drawn in by this family. They're all crazy. They'll make you crazy too.'

Before I can even process what Zara has said, I realise that Jack has stopped and is waiting for us. So the opportunity to respond to Zara vanishes immediately. As we walk on silently, I glance at Zara out of the corner of my eye. Why would she say that to me, if there wasn't something behind it? Maybe she was pranking me? Or perhaps, as Patrick's adult stepdaughter, she's found it hard to find a place for herself amongst the Silvers.

As we continue to walk along the snowy path, Zara's words of warning are ringing in my ears:

Don't get too drawn in by this family. They're all crazy. They'll make you crazy too.

Chapter Sixteen

Yasmin

In the end, we're outside for almost a whole hour. I'm glad I wrapped Lily up in plenty of layers, but her cheeks and nose are bright red and I worry she'll get a chill after that excursion. I carry my baby through to the lounge and pop her in the middle of the floor. I then set to work, opening the door of the wood burner, throwing in some kindling and lighting a match. I watch as the pieces of paper start to burn first, before the flames begin to lick the wooden logs beneath. I hurriedly shut the door, remembering Alicia's brush with fire the previous evening.

Lily is rolling around, trying to crawl and failing because her snow-suit is so bulky. I go to her rescue and help her out of her outdoor wear. She's immediately on the floor, making a beeline for the Christmas baubles once more.

'Lily, I said leave those alone!'

I'm too late this time, though. Lily swats a bauble off its branch and it crashes to the ground, shattering on the hard wooden floor. She reacts by making a small squeaking sound.

'Are you okay, baby?' I scoop her up and check her fingers for any broken shards, but she's been lucky and isn't hurt. I kiss her on the forehead. 'That's why we don't go near the tree,' I tell her. I want to be cross with her, but how can I when she looks so adorable?

Dawn swans into the room, looking flustered. 'Have you seen—' She freezes, her sight landing on the broken bauble. 'What happened?!' she exclaims, rushing towards the Christmas tree and hurling herself down on her knees.

'Lily knocked a bauble off the tree. I'll clear it up.'

Dawn begins sobbing.

I'm taken aback by her tears. 'It's only a bauble.'

'That wasn't... only a bauble...' Dawn sobs dramatically again. 'It was my grandmother's... a family heirloom.'

Oh no. It wasn't just a bauble after all then.

'This set of baubles has been in my family for three generations!'

'I'm sorry, Dawn. It was an accident.'

'It was irreplaceable!' Dawn has stood up now and is shouting. 'Every year I unbox those precious ornaments. And every year they're a comforting reminder of my grandmother and my mother!'

'What's going on?' Patrick has marched into the room, swiftly followed by Ronan. 'What's all the noise about?'

Dawn is crying uncontrollably now. I can't believe she's making such a fuss. Lily's a child. It was an accident.

'Lily knocked a bauble off the tree and it broke,' I explain, as patiently as I can. 'Dawn is upset as the bauble was part of a set belonging to her late grandmother.'

I hope I've explained the situation as calmly as possible. But now Lily is wriggling in my arms, clearly distressed by the scene Dawn is making.

'I'm sorry,' I say again, a little louder now so Dawn can hear me above her sobbing.

'Honestly,' Patrick says. 'I thought something terrible had happened.'

Dawn looks aghast at her husband. 'Something terrible *has* happened.' She looks hurt and put out that Patrick isn't at her side and making a fuss over her.

'She's only little,' Ronan adds. 'Lily didn't mean it.'

'That's not going to bring my bauble back, is it!' Dawn storms out of the room and stomps up the stairs. I'm beginning to see where Zara gets her stroppiness from.

'I'm so sorry,' I say to Patrick. 'I turned around for two seconds—'

Patrick puts his hand up to me to stop my sentence. 'Don't worry, it can't be helped. Children will be children.' He ruffles Lily's hair and then backtracks out of the room. To my surprise, he doesn't follow Dawn. Instead, he disappears into the kitchen.

I'm pretty sure that Patrick wouldn't be quite so blasé if something of his had been broken, but I'm relieved he seems relaxed about what happened. I can never quite tell what's going to set Patrick off. But at least this hasn't.

'Is Lily okay?' Ronan asks.

'She's fine.' I hand her over to Ronan and then I follow Patrick into the kitchen, in search of a dustpan and brush.

Alicia and Zara are at the breakfast bar. They're sharing a bowl of popcorn and chatting away to each other. Alicia gives me one of her silly little waves as I enter the room. I give her a tight smile back. I root around in the kitchen cupboards, looking for the dustpan. Alicia and Zara are talking about a TV show they've both watched. They seem to be getting very pally, pally all of a sudden. I must admit, I didn't see that coming. Zara's usual mode is sullen and reserved. So it's weird to see her chatting away like a normal human being. I always thought Zara was antisocial. But maybe she's not? Maybe I haven't made enough of an effort with her?

I finally locate the dustpan and brush and hurry back to the lounge. I examine the shards to see if they're salvageable, but the Christmas decoration looks damaged beyond repair. I carefully brush the pieces into a pan and wonder if there's anything at all I could do to fix this.

'Ouch, that's pretty broken,' Ronan comments over my shoulder.

'Do you think there's any way you could mend it?' Ronan likes a project, but his restorations tend to be on a much bigger scale than this.

'I'm not sure...' He thinks for a minute. 'Let me take it, and I'll see what I can do.'

We do a swapsie and Ronan takes the shattered bauble away and I'm holding Lily once more. She snuggles into me.

'It's okay, it was an accident,' I repeat to my little girl as I rub her back.

I sit down in one of the squashy armchairs. After the long walk and the drama, I feel exhausted. I wrap my arms around my daughter. She's probably tired after all that fresh air. The heat from the fire warms me and I let my mind wander.

I think back over my relationship with Dawn. When did things start to change? Ronan and I got together ten years ago, we've been married for seven. Whereas Dawn came into Patrick's life about six years ago. They were married after a year and they recently celebrated their fifth wedding anniversary in Italy this summer. Therefore, I have almost an extra half a decade of history with the Silver men. Half a decade of knowledge of Patrick, Ronan and Jack. I listen to the fire crackling and spitting in the hearth. The sound soothes me as I sort through a jumble of memories.

At first, Dawn was more than friendly with me. She showered me with affection and was over the top in her attempts to form a connection between us. We'd meet up for coffees, afternoon teas, trips to the theatre. She became a friend, a confidante. I encouraged her relationship with Patrick. Gave her advice on the gifts to buy him and informed her of his passions and interests.

Patrick fell head over heels for Dawn. She's charismatic, energetic, bubbly. She filled his house with laughter and flattered him at every turn. She made herself irresistible to him and he fell for it. Hook, line and sinker.

They got engaged swiftly. I recall Patrick saying that, at his time of life, there was no point in waiting around. He had to grab every opportunity with both hands and he certainly did that with Dawn. Their OTT displays of affection were cringe-worthy at points. I didn't care too much – it wasn't my mother or father. Ronan turned a blind eye. The thing my husband wants most in life is to be in his father's good books. It fuels everything he does, every decision he makes. He saw Patrick was happy and, more importantly, he recognised that his father's mind was made up about Dawn. So he supported their relationship wholeheartedly.

Jack, on the other hand, wasn't so pleased with the turn of events and wasn't overly welcoming to Dawn. He had a close bond with his own mother. He blamed his father for his parents' messy divorce and claimed that it ruined his mother's life. In turn, he cited stress as the cause for her early heart attack. She died at just fifty-two years old, when Jack and Ronan were in their early twenties.

It was tragic. I knew their mother, albeit very briefly. She was a troubled woman, with many demons. Drink being one of them. So, in some ways, her sudden death wasn't as much of a surprise as it could have been. But Jack was hit hard by it, completely devastated. It didn't help that Patrick refused to attend the funeral, even though he paid for it. It was a strange time and a gulf definitely grew between Patrick and Jack. Their relationship has never fully recovered. They're still distant with each other now.

But Dawn and I had been close, up until recently. In the last year, things have changed. Maybe that's because I've changed so much. Or maybe Dawn is jealous of the attention Patrick gives to my daughter.

I guess one of the reasons why I didn't extend the hand of friendship to Zara was because Dawn and I were spending so much time together. Zara does her own thing; she has her canal boat and is often off on adventures in the vessel she'd named *Petal*. I didn't see much of her and she's always kept herself to herself so far. From what I can gather, she only sees Dawn on holidays or birthdays.

Alicia and Zara appear in the lounge and I sit bolt upright, one arm around Lily. Lily is sound asleep by now. I had been nodding off as well and my eyes feel heavy and gritty. I sigh.

'Sorry, did we wake you?' Alicia asks sweetly.

'No, no, it's okay,' my voice is a whisper as I don't want to disturb Lily. 'I was just resting my eyes.'

Alicia and Zara look awkwardly at one another; Zara is clutching a big bowl of popcorn.

'Don't mind us,' I say, rising from the chair still cradling my daughter. 'I'm going to go and put Lily in her cot for half an hour.'

I exit the room and overhear Alicia and Zara discussing what movies they want to watch. They're sounding very cosy indeed. And given Dawn's shift in our alliance, I can't help feeling frustrated with the turn of events. I'm usually at the heart of the goings-on in this family. I was the glue that kept Patrick, Ronan and Jack together through hard times, way before Dawn was on the scene. There were a lot of difficult conversations and emotions running between Patrick and Jack. Who put all the hard work in to make sure they kept communicating? Who spent hours of her time consoling Jack? Who helped Patrick to move on? *All me.*

So I'm not prepared to feel pushed out and excluded from the little friendship that's forming between Alicia and Zara – or for either of them to reshape the dynamics of this family. And I'm definitely not going to stand for Dawn shouting at me and my daughter. It was noticeable Patrick leapt to my defence. He knows how much I've done for this family.

I need to go and think about how to handle things. Work out my next move and make sure that Alicia and Zara don't get too close. Because I don't want Alicia making herself too comfortable.

As I'm going to make sure that she doesn't keep the name Mrs Silver for very long.

Chapter Seventeen

Alicia

I'm having a blissful time today. This is what Christmas is all about – kicking back and relaxing, lounging on the sofa, eating way too many chocolates and enjoying a festive film. I seem to have found an unexpected friend. Zara is more than happy to accompany me as we sit together on the expensive sofa, in the luxurious lounge, drinking posh wine and eating upmarket crisps. We chose a golden-oldie favourite to begin with, easy watching, a beautiful romance, a few giggles and a hero who's easy on the eye. What more could you want from a festive movie?

The wood burner has made the room feel toasty and relaxed. Without the others around, I feel less on edge and I don't have to watch everything I say or do. Dawn is still upstairs, Yasmin's with Lily, and the men have disappeared outside on their quest for more logs. There's been no more snow but I have no desire to go back out into the cold. I'm glad Patrick, Jack and Ronan have taken on that task so I can stay inside the lodge.

After chatting to Zara for a good few hours solid, during the walk, over an impromptu lunch of crackers and cheese, and whilst we've been half watching the film, I'm relieved that I now have a partner-in-crime. I was worried that I just wouldn't find anyone amongst the Silver brood who I had anything in common with. But Zara and I are getting on brilliantly now that the ice has been broken and we've both opened up a little more. The wine, along with the lack of interference from anyone else, has helped.

I top up our wine glasses and settle back down amongst the cushions. The movie being played out on the screen has nearly come to an end. Zara and I watch the romantic ending before the closing credits run.

'That was just perfect,' I declare, brandishing my wine glass in the air, a little bit of the clear liquid sloshing over the side. I right my glass quickly, but Zara doesn't seem to care.

'Exactly how the Christmas holidays are meant to be spent.'

'I couldn't agree more.' I sit up in the chair and check my watch. 'I wonder when the menfolk will be back.'

'Aww, are you missing Jack already?' Zara teases.

I flush.

'You are, aren't you?' Zara sighs. 'So, is Jack the one – your true love – just like in the movies?'

'Of course he is! I married him.'

'Marriage doesn't necessarily equal love,' Zara responds darkly.

I stare at her. I'm not sheltered enough to think that every marriage ends in a love story, but I know I could never have said my vows if I didn't think Jack was the person that I wanted to spend the rest of my life with. There are plenty of reasons for marriage, but I'm a complete romantic. It's why I held out for Jack for so long. I was totally besotted with him from the first time we met. It may have taken him a while to notice it and even longer than that to return my feelings, but he loves me now, I'm sure of that. I've got my happily-ever-after.

'What's your love life like?' I ask Zara, sensing a sadness in this area for her.

'Oh, don't ask. It's a long story.'

'We're snowed in, in an isolated lodge in the Irish mountains. I've got plenty of time!'

Zara smiles weakly. 'There's not too much to say.' She sighs heavily. 'I've never been lucky in love. Scratch that, I've never been lucky full stop.'

'Your time will come,' I reassure her. Having spent a few hours with her, it's clear that Zara lacks confidence.

'Not sure about that...' Zara drinks deeply. 'Not everyone can have a fairy-tale romance.' She purses her lips and falls silent.

'Is there someone you have feelings for?'

Zara looks up at me, her eyes moist. 'Not anymore.' She looks away and composes herself. 'The truth is, the only man who's ever truly loved me is my daddy.'

I'm not sure what the background is between Zara's parents, but I'm guessing it's not happy as Dawn is now married to Patrick. However, I'm not ready for what Zara says next.

'My dad died in a house fire.'

I gasp. 'Oh my God! You poor thing, that's horrendous!' I move closer to Zara and put a hand on her shoulder. 'I'm so sorry, I had no idea.'

'It's okay, no one ever mentions it. It's like his memory has been erased... totally forgotten, like he was never here.' A single tear drops down Zara's cheek.

'That must have been so hard for you.'

Zara looks surprised at my reaction.

'What was he like?' I ask her.

Zara stutters, 'You're the first person in a long time who's asked me that question.' She uses the back of her hand to swipe away some tears before continuing. 'He was generous, and funny, and gave the best hugs.'

I give Zara a squeeze at this; I can feel myself welling up. 'I'm here any time you want to talk to me about him.'

'Thanks. That's nice of you.'

'Does your mum never talk about him?'

'My mum?' Zara looks at me confused.

'Yeah, does Dawn not have photos at home or...'

'Dawn isn't my mum,' Zara says flatly.

Now it's my turn to look confused.

'Dawn is my stepmother. She married my father when I was fourteen. My biological mother did a disappearing act when I was little. So Dawn is the closest thing to family I have. I don't see her all that often nowadays, just birthdays and Christmases. When she married Patrick, she insisted that I joined in this annual Christmas holiday charade.' Zara looks away, out the window. 'To be honest, I wasn't going to bother coming this year. I always feel like an outsider.'

'I know that feeling,' I say, trying to take in everything Zara has just revealed.

'It's a good job I came, though,' Zara says, a note of brightness in her voice. 'Because now I've met you.'

Zara says this with such feeling that I'm taken aback. We've only been chatting properly today. I'm pleased Zara is here to spend some time with, but I can't imagine us being bosom buddies in the outside world, away from this family set up.

'Jack has always been kind to me,' Zara continues. 'Maybe we can form our own breakaway family.' She laughs, a little manically. The effects of the wine are clearly coming into play.

I don't mean to do it so obviously but I find myself edging away from her a little. Putting some space between the two of us. There's something about the intense way she's looking at me that startles me. After all, we don't know each other that well and I don't want Zara forming some big attachment to me. Then again, I do feel sorry for her. Perhaps she just needs a friend in the world.

Zara is still staring out of the window, in her own little world. I look out at the snowy scene in front of us. It looks so serene and pretty. And then my husband appears over the crest of the hill in front of the house. My handsome Jack, wearing a black padded coat, dark waterproof trousers and sturdy walking boots. And he looks so sexy. I'm glad he has returned, as things are starting to get a bit heavy with Zara.

I head to the front door and fling it open, greeting my husband, his brother and my father-in-law. They've got a sack truck filled with logs.

'I'll go round the back with this,' Ronan says, indicating to the logs.

'Would you like a hot drink?' I suggest to Jack.

'Music to my ears!' He grins. 'But I'd like a kiss first.' We smooch on the doorstep, just under the hanging mistletoe.

I feel like the luckiest woman in the world.

***

After stocking up on drinks and snacks, Jack and I head into the lounge. Zara seems to have shaken off her melancholy and there's no sign of her tears. We flick through the festive offerings on the TV and settle on a game show. I'm now curled up on the sofa, my head resting on Jack's arm. The clock on the mantelpiece ticks round another hour. I feel relaxed and drowsy.

At some point, Patrick comes and sits in the armchair, Nuala finds a spot at his feet and both of them, man and dog, snore away together in the corner of the room. There's still no sign of Dawn – she hasn't come downstairs since her earlier outburst. Ronan, Yasmin and Lily are all in the kitchen. They're enjoying some time together as a trio. Yasmin had some colouring pencils and paper out and was encouraging Lily to scribble with them.

As I recline on the sofa, Jack's fingers lightly smooth my hair, gently caressing my forehead and making me feel even sleepier. I switch off from the programme on the TV and think about the first time I saw Jack. We were both on a graduate scheme at a finance company. It was our first day there and Jack was wearing a smart grey suit. It was love at first sight for me. There was just something about the way he stood so confidently, the playful look in his eyes, and the deep cadence to his voice. It was the first and only time I've fallen in love.

Jack, however, was oblivious to my feelings. Our paths crossed now and again during working hours but the conversation rarely strayed into anything meaningful. I was struggling in my role and I realised quite quickly that the job wasn't for me. But my parents were so proud of me, so I vowed to stick it out for the year. It helped that Jack was there – he was my reason for getting up and out of bed in the morning.

My time at the company was drawing to a close and it was looking like I'd never get to know Jack properly. That was until a mutual friend threw a Halloween party. Jack went as a vampire and I went as a vamp.

Afterwards, he told me it was the fishnet stockings that caught his attention. But whatever it was, that night was the best of my life. Jack and I spent all night talking and from there things developed. We began to pop to the pub in the evenings together, we'd occasionally meet for a long walk or a Sunday lunch. The connection between us remained undefined. I'd seen plenty of friends pressuring the guys they wanted to be with into relationships, even into proposals. I wasn't in any hurry to race down the aisle and I wanted things to develop at their own pace. I just wanted to spend time with Jack.

Except years went by and nothing changed. We were never officially girlfriend and boyfriend, although he was always by my side at my birthday celebrations, he'd whisk me away on mini-breaks and buy me thoughtful presents. But there was no declaration of love from him.

I never put too much pressure on him, though, because I was prepared to wait, my feelings were so strong for him. It's odd, as in my twenties I launched a business and I classed myself as an independent woman. I have a great group of friends, an income of my own and yet, when it came to Jack, all rational thought went out the window. I did have a wobble as I hit thirty. I was convinced I'd made a mistake by playing the long game with Jack Silver. And I was worried I was missing my opportunity for a proper relationship elsewhere. I couldn't help how I felt about him, though. It was so easy to say 'yes' when he called me up and asked if I was free to go on a road trip. Or when he knocked at my door late at night for a booty call. I was powerless to say no to him.

I made a snap decision to go travelling, first to Thailand and then I extended my trip to a full six months. I went to Cambodia and Vietnam and ended with a short stint in America, the final week in

New York. I wasn't intending to go to America at all, but on my travels I made a great friend, Leah Bailey, and we hit it off, spending the last three months of my trip together. She convinced me to go to America with her for a few weeks, before we travelled back to England together. She was returning to the UK for a short stint to see family prior to a big adventure in Australia.

I'd told her all about Jack and my increasing doubts about whether we'd ever be a proper couple. Leah advised me not to get back to his messages so quickly – if at all. And to play the social media game, showing all my followers – including Jack – what an amazing time I was having. I did exactly that and, to my surprise, Jack was waiting at the airport to pick me up when I landed at London Gatwick, with a big bunch of a dozen red roses in his hands. It was so romantic. I remember Leah giving me a knowing wink as we parted at the airport, as if to say: *See, my advice worked*.

I'll never know whether it was her advice on the tactics to employ to keep men interested that did the trick or whether it was just a case of absence making the heart grow fonder, but I owe Leah either way. It was a shame she couldn't make it to our wedding, as she was in Oz at the time, but we still keep in touch.

From the minute I touched down on English soil, things rapidly changed between Jack and I. He suggested marriage on the night of my return. I hesitated, wondering if he really meant it. We spent the first few weeks of me being back in England in a little bubble, mostly in bed, and after a few weeks, Jack had whisked me away to Paris, gone down on one knee and proposed to me for a second time with a beautiful ring.

Zara is right, I do have my very own happy ending. I just hope it stays this way forever.

Patrick gets up. 'I'm just going to see where Dawn is,' he announces to nobody in particular. Nuala pads after him.

I get up and nip to the loo. I feel a little nauseous. I think it might be laying in the warm room for so long and possibly the number of glasses of wine I've consumed as well. So I open the front door and stand just outside it for a bit. My head is spinning, so I breathe in big lungfuls of the clean, fresh air. Snowflakes are beginning to fall again and the clouds above look dark and ominous.

Gradually, the feeling passes. I'm not sure how long I've been standing outdoors, but I do feel a bit better. I turn to make my way inside and walk straight into Jack.

'What are you doing out there?'

'Just getting a bit of air.' My teeth are chattering, I hadn't realised how cold it was. The door shuts softly behind me.

'You're freezing!' Jack says, pulling me to him and rubbing my arms with his hands.

I inhale the familiar scent of his aftershave and lay my head on his chest. I close my eyes. When I open them again, I see Yasmin at the other end of the hallway. She's standing on the other side of the partially closed kitchen door and she's looking straight at me, her brown eyes staring through the gap of open space. She retreats backwards, as though she didn't mean for me to notice her.

I shiver. Something about the way she looked at me felt cold and threatening. I'm suspicious of my sister-in-law and my gut instinct is not to trust her.

I tug at Jack's hand and we make our way back to the comfort of the lounge and the warmth of the roaring fire. We settle down again, and I lay along the sofa with my feet in Jack's lap. We both relax, a comedy show now playing on the TV. Zara laughs on the other side of the room. This is exactly what the Christmas holidays should be about: laughter, comfort and absolutely nothing to worry over.

But all that was about to change...

***

Half an hour later, the peace and quiet is shattered when the door slams open. 'Which one of you was it?' Patrick rages into the room. 'Which one of you was it?' He repeats the same sentence again, this time even louder.

Jack and I sit up rapidly. This is the first time I've seen Patrick properly angry, and the sight of him scares me.

'What's going on?' Jack replies, a look of puzzlement on his face.

'Who did it? Who locked her out?'

'What are you talking about?' Jack says, standing up now.

'Someone locked my Nuala outside!'

Yasmin and Ronan both rush into the room and stop abruptly when they see the expression on Patrick's face.

'Are you okay, Dad?' Ronan asks.

'No, I'm not. Someone locked Nuala outside and now she's a shaking mess. If anything happens to her...'

The threat is left hanging in the air.

The whimpering, wet dog limps slowly into the room.

Zara drops to her knees, pulls her black jumper off in one swift movement and wraps it around the shaking animal.

'Calm down, Dad,' Jack says gently.

'I will not calm down! She could've died out there!'

'Alicia, did you see Nuala when you went outside earlier?' Yasmin's eyes are narrowed and her voice is accusing.

'No,' I reply immediately, because that's the truth.

'You went outside?' Patrick whirls around to face me.

'Yes,' I reply meekly. 'But Nuala wasn't out there and I didn't see her—'

'Has anyone else been outside?' Patrick shouts to the room, his cheeks are red and his eyes are blazing. I've never seen someone look so mad or frightening before.

There's no response from anyone else. This is excruciating. But I'm certain Nuala wasn't outside the front door when I was standing out there. I didn't see her slip by me at any point and I'm pretty sure I would have noticed. I open my mouth to protest, but then I see the way Patrick is looking at me. Anything I say now could potentially make things ten times worse.

'Oh Alicia, it's not your fault. You're not used to having a dog,' Yasmin says, her eyebrow arched as she's talking.

I'm shocked, Yasmin is throwing me under the bus and she knows it.

I look towards Jack – why hasn't he said anything? He's just hanging his head and I notice his hands are balled into tight fists at his side. Is he angry at me or his father?

The silence is deafening. Everyone has their eyes on me.

'I'm sorry, I didn't see Nuala outside, but of course I apologise if she somehow got out when I was...' My voice tails off. I'm trying to keep myself calm and respond in a reasonable way to this accusation. I hope I strike the balance between standing up for myself but also apologising, as it seems it's the only thing I can do right now. Everyone in this room must think I let the dog out.

Patrick huffs loudly but seems to deflate a little. He turns around to exit the room and Jack is standing by the door. As Patrick passes his eldest son, I hear him say, 'I hope you've made the right decision marrying her.'

My eyes sting with tears and my throat burns.

Yasmin throws me a sly look and then retreats from the room, following Patrick and Ronan.

'Jack—' I start to say.

'Let's talk upstairs,' he replies sharply. And then my husband also stalks off.

I'm left feeling shell-shocked about what's just happened and indignant that the finger of blame was pointed at me.

'I told you to be careful.'

I jump.

Zara is still sitting on the sofa, and she repeats her warning again. 'I told you to be careful. Watch your back. Yasmin is poisonous.'

I think Zara might be right.

My sister-in-law hates me, but why?

Chapter Eighteen

Jack

I rush up the stairs, taking them two at a time, and dive into my bedroom as quickly as possible. What a shambles tonight was. Yesterday evening was bad, but I think today's scene may have even topped that. It's been a long time since I've seen my father quite that mad. He absolutely adores Nuala. The dog has been part of the family for eight years now and my father takes her everywhere with him. So I'm not surprised he reacted in the way he did.

I sit down on the edge of the bed and put my head in my hands. I'm annoyed that Alicia got wrapped up in the drama, though. Did she really not see the dog outside? She's the only person that I've noticed going out the front door this afternoon since my father, Ronan and I came back from collecting the logs. I have no idea how long she was standing by the door for, but she was dazed enough when I found her that it's possible that she may have missed Nuala escaping.

I'm relieved Alicia didn't mention I was the one who shut the door when she came back inside. There's no doubt my father would've raged at me too if he'd discovered that piece of information. I'm grateful to her for not saying anything, but I'm also frustrated that she's managed to rub everyone up the wrong way again. What is she doing? Is it because she's still nervous? Or is she doing it on purpose?

Before the last couple of days, I didn't have any hesitations in bringing Alicia to spend the Christmas holidays with my family. She's usually so presentable and dependable. She's never one to draw attention to herself or cause arguments. I thought she'd slot right in. Something must be up.

A sudden thought hits me and my stomach flips. Perhaps she's found out why I really married her?

I stand up and move towards the window, looking out at the cold, unforgiving mountain. She can't have discovered my motives yet, can she? I bite my lip, trying to think how she might have uncovered my secrets. And then a slow, creeping sense of unease washes over me. Alicia has been talking a lot to Zara today. But that doesn't mean anything... does it?

The door opens behind me and the woman who is now my wife steps softly into the bedroom.

'Jack? Jack, I'm so sorry.'

I turn around and study Alicia's face. It's creased with worry and her eyes are brimming with unshed tears. This isn't the face of someone who's found out her marriage is a lie and her husband didn't marry her for love. I exhale, my shoulders dropping. I think the truth is still under wraps, for now.

'Alicia, did you see Nuala outdoors?' My words sound harsher than I meant them to.

Alicia sits down on the bed. She shakes her head furiously, 'No, Jack. I didn't.'

'Okay.' I sit down next to her, my heart beating fast.

I don't think she'd lie to me. She's been besotted with me since we first met. Even though I wasn't immediately drawn to her, our casual arrangement has been convenient over the years. Alicia never put any demands on me. She never pressured me into making our relationship official or exclusive like so many of my friends' partners. She seemed happy to go with the flow and just enjoy the time when we were together. It was easy for us to fall into a rhythm. If I was at a loose end or wanting company, then I knew Alicia would be there. We went through phases of behaving as though we were in a serious relationship. We went on sun-drenched holidays together, we did our weekly shopping hand-in-hand, went for meals during the week and spent whole weekends in each other's flats. She's easy company as well as being very pretty. I do care about her and we have lots of shared history now. There's just a certain spark that's missing and I never wanted commitment. Many of my friends urged me to make an honest woman of Alicia, and now I have – but not for the reasons she'd hoped.

After living through my own parents' marriage, I vowed I'd never get tied down by anyone and I promised myself that I'd never walk down the aisle, because it seemed like the path to certain misery. But all that had to change. And Alicia was the obvious choice for me, even if I don't love her in the way that I should.

'Jack, why didn't you stand up for me?' Alicia says, a tremor in her voice which brings me back to the present.

'What?'

'Why didn't you say that you saw me outside and you shut the door when I came back in? Because that's the truth and it may have stopped your father being so angry at me.'

Alicia looks sad and dejected. I have a split second of feeling sorry for putting her through what I have. I should never have dragged her into my complicated family.

'Alicia...' I should apologise and say that I agree with her, but I can't. 'Alicia, I only saw you briefly. You'd been outside for a while; I didn't check out there myself because I didn't think you'd miss my father's dog being out in the snow!'

'I didn't see Nuala!' Alicia protests. Her eyes are shining now. 'I didn't see the dog because she wasn't out there when I was. Why won't anyone believe me?'

'Because you're the only one that's been outside this afternoon,' I bite back.

'Am I?'

'Well, no one else—'

'No one else would own up to it, though, would they. Not with Patrick being as irate as he was. I've been on the sofa in the lounge with Zara for most of the afternoon. Yet no one else has been interrogated. You didn't defend me either. And Yasmin was very quick to accuse me...'

Alicia's words rush out, she's fired up and hurt. I've only seen her like this once or twice in the whole time I've known her. So I need to tread carefully as I don't want her to go off the deep end about this. And I don't want her to say the wrong thing in front of everyone else.

'Alicia...' I go to take her hand in mine, but she pulls away.

'We're meant to be a team now, Jack.' She runs to the bathroom and closes the door firmly shut behind her.

We haven't had an argument since our marriage. And we've only ever had small disagreements or minor cross words in all the time we've known each other. Alicia is usually low-maintenance. This is new; this is one of the reasons why I didn't want to get locked into a marital relationship in the first place.

I give her a few minutes and then gently knock on the door.

'Are you okay?'

Alicia eventually allows me into the bathroom, her face is tear-stained and her eyes are puffy.

'Come here,' I say, and she falls into my arms.

'Your family hates me,' Alicia sobs.

'Hates you? No they don't,' I try to reassure her. 'They just don't know you very well yet, that's all. They're going to love you, I know it.' I can only hope that I'm right. I thought it would be simple to get my family to like Alicia, but now I realise it's going to take more effort. I need to do more. 'I don't want to argue,' I say to my wife, tipping her chin up so that she's looking at me.

'Me neither,' she replies, wiping her eyes with her sleeves.

'Things will feel better in the morning.' I wrap her in my arms and we stay like that for a while.

As we stand there, listening to the clock ticking in the background and staring out the big, glass window to the snowy landscape beyond, I'm debating something in my mind. Should I let Alicia in on a family secret? Maybe if she's in the know, then things might be easier?

'I don't think Yasmin likes me very much,' Alicia says eventually.

This is it. This is my opportunity to share an important jigsaw piece of information with Alicia, so she can get a better understanding of the picture of my family and the truth behind the expensive clothes and the upper-class accents.

'There's something I need to tell you,' I say, uncertainly.

'What is it?' Alicia's eyes are big and round.

I hesitate. I have no idea how she might react to what I'm about to say. Once I've said it, there's no going back.

'Jack, you can tell me anything. I'm your wife.'

I take her hands in mine. And then I whisper something to her, something that will change her view of the Silver family forever.

Alicia's face falls.

Have I misjudged this? Can I trust her?

Chapter Nineteen

Now

The Garda burst through the door, dragging me in their wake. My hands are tightly cuffed behind my back.

I'm shaking. Numb with shock.

A voice says, 'What's going on?'

There's silence. I look up to see a familiar pair of eyes staring back at me.

'What's going on?' The question is repeated. I wish I knew the answer.

The oldest officer steps forward. He has a grey beard and grey eyes. I don't catch his reply.

I can't seem to focus on the exchange pinging back and forth.

My mind wanders. None of us thought it would be so difficult to find Dawn.

I gulp down my emotions.

Will joining that search party be the biggest mistake of my life?

Chapter Twenty

Yasmin

Urgh. I wake up to the sound of Lily crying and peel my face off the pillow. My hair is matted and my eyes are gritty with sleep dust. I glance over at Ronan. He's snoring his head off and oblivious to our child is currently screaming the house down. I sigh.

'It's okay, Lily, I'm coming,' I say into her baby monitor. Then I pad quickly across the hall and into the little bedroom that has been kitted out for her.

Lily is standing up in her cot, snot streaming out of her nose and mixing with the tears running down her flushed cheeks. I grab a bib and wipe her face clean before picking her up.

'Poor baby,' I say. 'What's the matter?'

I rock her side to side, thinking it will be so much easier when she can talk and tell me what's wrong. She snuggles into me and her eyelids begin to flutter. After just a few minutes, she has fallen back to sleep. I very carefully place her back down on her mattress. I stand by the side of the cot, lingering for longer than I need to, just to make sure she is properly settled. I tiptoe out of the room and a floorboard creaks. I hold my breath. But there's no reaction from my daughter. She's sleeping soundly now.

I go back to my own room and lay down again, pulling the covers up around me and willing myself to go straight back to sleep. But I'm wide awake now and mundane thoughts are circling my mind. A tick list of things I need to do to get me and Lily ready in the morning, a number of niggling tasks that have to be done as soon as I return to work and general life admin that seems to have piled up in the last few weeks. I went all in for Lily's first Christmas and we have seen Santa at least three times. That's not to mention the Christmas-themed sensory class, music class and messy play class. We also went to the Dublin Castle Christmas market and met with various friends for meals and drinks out across December. I'm usually very social across the year, with a packed diary, but Christmastime is especially busy as both Ronan and I have December birthdays. So it truly is a month of celebrations. I've loved every minute of our days and nights out, but it has been much more tiring doing it all with a baby. Then my thoughts turn to our Christmas holiday. It's been quite drama-filled so far – not exactly quiet or relaxing.

Eventually, I must have drifted off. But it only feels like twenty minutes later and Ronan's alarm is bleeping. I roll over and bury my head in the pillow.

Ronan jumps straight out of bed, as he always does on hearing his wake-up alarm, and stretches, flinging his arms wide. He growls and says, 'I always sleep so well in that bed. We might have to get the same mattress for our house.'

I don't respond. I hate it when Ronan wakes up all fresh, with no realisation that Lily has woken me in the night. As Ronan disappears into the bathroom, I close my eyes for fifteen short minutes, enjoying the lie-in as Lily is still sleeping.

'I'm heading down for breakfast,' Ronan tells me now that he's showered. 'You better get moving.' Ronan is rushing about because Patrick runs a well-ordered ship. Mealtimes are like clockwork and everything in Patrick's world has a time slot allocated throughout the day. Normally, I don't mind this at all but after almost a year of sleepless nights, I could do with a proper break.

I rub my eyes; I don't feel great. My temperature is running slightly too warm and my throat feels scratchy. I move to sit up but there's a sharp pain in my abdomen, followed by a dull familiar ache. I make my way slowly to the bathroom and, just as I suspected, my period has kicked in.

I feel deflated. I was hopeful that Ronan and I had conceived. But it looks like I've jumped to conclusions too quickly and both my husband and Patrick are going to be disappointed.

I'm disappointed too. Ronan and I have been trying for another child for almost six months now. I worry that falling pregnant isn't going to be as easy the second time around. But I push the thought to one side before I get sucked into a spiral of worry.

I look at myself in the mirror. My face is drained of colour and looks slightly grey. I shake myself. I need to perk up and get ready for the day. I can't let the arrival of my period bring me down. I need to continue to keep my favour with Patrick firmly in place. And I need to be on form this week. I grab my extortionately expensive face scrub and my bamboo face cloth and set to work invigorating my tired skin.

I decide that I'm not going to mention to Ronan that I'm not pregnant, or Patrick for that matter. I knew yesterday that if I shared my inkling to Ronan of the possibility of me being pregnant, then he would go and announce it to the whole family. Because that's exactly what my husband is like: he can't keep a secret. And he also can't help but broadcast whatever's on his mind.

It doesn't hurt for Patrick to believe he has another grandchild on the way soon. We've been trying and I'm hopeful that I will have another baby growing inside me in the not too distant future. Patrick is such a proud grandfather and he absolutely dotes on Lily. She's the apple of his eye. And she adores him back. A second grandchild would be the icing on the cake for my father-in-law.

This all helps with the plans that I've set in motion because I want to ensure that Ronan and I benefit completely from Patrick's will when the time comes. Yes, I know it's morbid to think of it, but I have my reasons. Patrick is loaded – his bank account runs into the millions – and I want to ensure that Ronan, Lily and I are set for life. And that doesn't involve things being split down the line with Jack or Dawn. After all, Jack rarely puts in the effort with Patrick. Ronan sees Patrick at least once a week, if not several times. They often meet for long lunches and business discussions, as well as pints of Irish cider in an old Irish pub in Dublin that's roughly halfway between our house and Patrick's. Whereas Jack might not see his father for months on end. Jack was more of a Mummy's boy, and his parents' divorce and his mother's subsequent early departure from this earth has always been a wedge between him and Patrick. I need to make sure that wedge between them stays in place.

I wasn't worried about Jack before he got married – I actively tried to heal the relationship between him and Patrick. But now my brother-in-law has a wife and could well be about to produce a few grandchildren with Alicia. And this worries me because it means Ronan and Lily's share of the inheritance will diminish.

And don't get me started on Dawn. It's obvious she's a gold-digger. She only wanted Patrick for one thing. I could curse myself for championing her in the early days of her courtship with Patrick. But I was young and naive back then. I know what there is to lose now. I'm not about to allow my husband and my daughter's fortunes to be ruined because of Patrick's wife, who drains his funds with constant fancy holidays and updates to their already enviable home.

I've worked hard over the last ten years to be the perfect wife and the perfect daughter-in-law. Dawn has been a problem that I've been working on ever since her attitude towards me changed. But I honestly thought that Jack would remain an eternal bachelor; I didn't envisage any competition from his quarter. I'm determined not to have all my hard work undone and I especially don't want to lose half of our fortune to someone as unrefined as Alicia. That's why I'm determined to get rid of her.

Ronan has let me into a few family secrets lately. Like how Patrick is starting to plan for his retirement and he wants to get his affairs in order too. Apparently, Patrick has asked Ronan to take the helm of his business when the time comes, so that's promising. Ronan was chuffed to bits to know that his father trusted him with his empire. My husband was also relieved that Patrick wasn't planning to sell out or leave the running of the business to shareholders. Ronan, of course, holds some shares already, I made sure of that years ago. Beyond that, he doesn't have much to do with the running of Patrick's business. So I'm proud of Ronan for his successful image and I'm also reassured that Patrick has recognised his second son's business talents. It bodes well for things to come.

But I don't want to leave anything to chance. Ronan doesn't forward plan as much as I do. This is the reason why the company accounts for our property business aren't looking as healthy as they should, which is something Patrick isn't aware of. When I came back to my role from maternity leave, I realised that Ronan had been struggling without my support. Our property empire has hit a few cash-flow issues in the last few months. It was unexpected, as things had been going so well.

Recently, I've also discovered there are more financial issues than Ronan had originally shared with me. He hadn't been entirely truthful about our lack of profits last year. He said he didn't want to worry me whilst I was pregnant or after Lily's birth. But I was still fuming with him for letting things get so bad and also for not telling me sooner.

I can't believe things have unravelled so quickly. If I'd known, I may have been able to do something to turn things around faster. Now I'm doing everything I can to try to make up for lost time and move us out of the red. No one suspects anything is wrong with the business, but it's only a matter of time until things spiral out of hand and we have to start shedding staff, or houses, or both. The embarrassment would be awful if it does have to come to that.

It's a tricky predicament to be in. The best solution would be to begin streamlining immediately, but Ronan wants to save face. He doesn't want any of his competitors or clients sussing out that something is up. And the last thing he wants is for his father to find out. His father's business has been so successful and Patrick has been enormously proud of Ronan striking out on his own and building a company from the ground up. Ronan is very good at schmoozing, bringing in new opportunities and projecting an outwardly impressive image, but unfortunately his business acumen doesn't stretch to the day-to-day running of things.

We really need to get a full-time manager in, someone who can help share my load and improve the current outlook. I've been trying to come up with outside-the-box solutions on who we could hire to help. Because if things don't miraculously make a recovery in the next few months, we could have a difficult time ahead of us. I've suggested to Ronan that we sell the business while we can still get away with being creative with the accounts in order to make a good sale. He's reluctant, but he's starting to come round to the idea.

Ultimately, it looks like we will have to close our business before it crumbles around us. So that's why I want to make sure that Ronan and Lily receive the lion's share of Patrick's inheritance. We'd be set for life and wouldn't have to worry about money ever again. We could eventually sell Patrick's company and live off the proceeds.

I've got to ensure my little family are given preference when it comes to Patrick's will. And I'm not going to let Dawn or Alicia stand in my way.

Chapter Twenty-One

Alicia

Jack and I kissed and made up last night. It had been a rollercoaster day, firstly with the accusation from Patrick over Nuala and then, later on, Jack divulged a shocking family secret with me. This morning, everything still feels off-kilter and weird between us. Yes, Jack shared something huge with me, which makes me think he must trust me. But he also didn't stand up for me or fight my corner yesterday, and that made me more upset than Patrick being angry with me.

We've never had a proper argument before. There have been a few little niggles over the years, but only about small things – nothing major. Since I came back from travelling, Jack has showered me with affection and I've felt as though his love for me was clear-cut. It seemed that, after years of building up to this point, Jack and I were finally a solid couple.

Well, that's what I thought until last night. Because how can I rely on him if he can't defend me when I need him to? The worst thing was, I think he doubted whether I was telling the truth. It was obvious that he wasn't convinced that I didn't let Nuala out the front door. So where does that leave me? And why did he then let me in on such a big secret after being so unsure about my actions during the day?

I'm probably reading far too much into his behaviour but the early days of our marriage are so important. These are the foundations that the rest of our lives will be built upon.

Everything feels intensified in this situation as well. It's like this pretty holiday lodge is in a snow globe that's been shaken up. Not only is the snow swirling all around us, but the emotions of everyone in the house are also being stirred up too. The gigantic windows in every room are meant to make you feel at one with nature. Except, with the looming mountain, the oppressive clouds and the expansive white landscape all around us, it feels more like I'm trapped here with no way out.

I sigh and sink into the bubble bath I've just run myself. I let my tense muscles relax and tell myself to let go of the argument. I don't want Jack and I to be having cross words while we're staying here, so I need to park my frustrations for now. I got up extra early this morning to get myself ready and downstairs for the start of breakfast. I could quite easily close my eyes and stay here for the remainder of the morning, in the peace and the quiet, where there's no tiptoeing around people or trying to avoid family dramas. But I've got a head start on the day, so I want to make the most of it. The early bird catches the worm and all that.

I dry myself quickly and get changed into the outfit that I've pre-selected. A long-sleeved plain white cotton T-shirt and thick, warm grey leggings coupled with an oversized black, white and grey checked shirt. I quickly dab on some make-up and survey myself in the still steamed-up mirror. I look just the part for a winter holiday in the mountains.

I slip on my wedding and engagement rings. The wedding ring is a beautiful gold band but the engagement ring is special on another level. It's an antique ruby red stone that's to die for. Jack said he saw it in a boutique jewellers in Brighton and it stood out to him. I can see why. It's an art deco piece that I would have picked out myself. A lot of my dress jewellery is in this style, and I can't believe I now have the real deal sitting on my ring finger. Jack didn't have any help choosing the engagement ring and it's perfect. It's things like this that make me believe that my husband really does know me and, more than that, he gets me too.

As I head back into the bedroom, Jack is still asleep. I sit down on my side of the bed and gaze at him. I still have to pinch myself at the thought of being Mrs Silver, Jack's wife. Only a year ago, I thought our time together had come to an end. When, really, it was just the beginning.

I wake him up with a kiss and he runs a hand through my strawberry-blonde hair, pulling me back down into the bed with him. Our argument last night seemingly forgotten by him. I'm relieved he isn't the sort of person to hold onto a grudge for long. And it's hard to stay angry with him when he's so sexy.

'Jack, I'm ready to go downstairs,' I protest. 'It's time to get up lazybones.'

He's undeterred and I lose my balance, falling back onto the pillow.

'Let's stay here today,' Jack murmurs groggily.

If only.

I hear the sound of someone on the landing outside and hop quickly out of bed. I want to start with the best impression I can today. I know I'm a people pleaser, but I can't help myself. Winning over Jack's family is the most important thing to me right now.

I pull away from Jack's enticing embrace and rush downstairs. As I enter the kitchen, the smell of good food hits my nostrils and it seems that the breakfast has been cooking for a while. Yasmin is at the coffee machine with Lily balanced on her hip and Dawn is bustling about at the stove. There's an icy tension between the two women. But when Dawn clocks me, she gives me a beaming smile.

'Good morning!' Dawn's voice is cheery, all trace of yesterday's tension has disappeared. 'We're having a full Irish breakfast today.'

'An Irish breakfast...' I've never had one before, so I'm curious as to what this consists of. 'What's in an Irish breakfast?'

Dawn chuckles. 'What isn't, more like! Patrick likes his with bacon rashers, fried egg, fried tomatoes, mushrooms, hash browns, soda bread and black pudding.' Dawn lists the items off on her fingers.

'Oh, so it is like an English breakfast then.'

Dawn raises her eyebrow at me. 'Don't let Patrick hear you say that! The difference is its Irish meat and Irish recipes. You won't say it's the same when you try the black pudding.' She smiles warmly at me to let me know that she's bantering with me.

'Coffee?' Yasmin cuts in abruptly.

'Err, no thanks.' I don't want to have to repeat my non-decaf preferences, so it's easier just to decline. 'Is there anything I can do?'

Yasmin is banging about with cups and utensils, clearly in a mood, whilst Dawn zooms around the kitchen preparing the first meal of the day.

'You could lay the table for me,' Dawn says. It strikes me this is the sort of task you'd give to a child or someone you didn't want near the oven, but I comply and go about finding the condiments and plates.

Yasmin plops Lily down in her high chair and gives the child a rusk to keep her entertained. Ronan and Patrick both filter into the room, with Nuala trailing after them. I flush when my father-in-law looks in my direction but he makes no comment about what happened yesterday and the dog seems fine now. Zara files into the room next, grey bags under her eyes, and she gives me a small nod before helping herself to a large mug of coffee.

Dawn begins bringing bowls and pans brimming with hot food to the table. So I help her to transfer everything from the kitchen area. Eventually, all the different breakfast options are in place and everyone is seated round the table and sorted with drinks. Jack saunters in just in time to take his seat next to me.

The chat this morning is mostly to do with business. I still don't really understand what Patrick does for work, so most of the conversation is going completely over my head. I think back to when I first met Jack at the finance company where we were graduates. The environment was way too corporate for my liking and there weren't many females in that company that made it to the top. After finishing my graduate scheme, I went onto a start-up company that was more forward-thinking and I thrived there. I loved every minute of the work I was doing and quickly rose up the ranks. After five happy years, I then felt that I had enough knowledge, and I'd made enough contacts, that I was ready to take the leap and set up my own business. I haven't looked back since. But what I'm doing is on a much, much smaller scale than either of Patrick or Ronan's companies.

I'm making peanuts in comparison to Patrick and Ronan's enterprises. Jack's salary, now he is on the board of directors, also outstrips what I'm bringing in every month. Although that doesn't really matter to me. I'm proud of how far I've come and the little company I've created all by myself. And it provides me with an enormous amount of flexibility. After four years of heading up my own company, I have enough processes in place and trusted freelancers contracted that I don't have to work at quite the same high intensity as when I first set the company up. This was the reason I was able to go away travelling for six months, still checking in on emails daily, but able to do my work from a golden beach or with the view of a famous landmark. I'm happy with how the work is ticking over now and I've managed to make a living for myself that I know my mum and dad would be proud of. And, in many ways, my little business has not only given me a stable income but it also set about the chain of events that led to Jack and I getting married.

'How's your work going, Alicia?' Dawn asks me, as though she is honing in on my thoughts.

I appreciate how much my new stepmother-in-law is trying to include me in things.

'Good, thank you. I'm not back until the eighth of January, so I have a nice stretch of holiday. I have a team in place who are safe hands while I'm off.'

'Good for you,' Dawn replies. 'You certainly seem like you've got your work/life balance in order.

'The hours were long when I first set up, but things are ticking over nicely now.'

'Well done, you.' Dawn tucks into a forkful of mushrooms.

I take a sip of my orange juice, feeling a little glow that something is going right.

'You don't want to get too complacent.' Patrick's gruff voice pops my little bubble of pride.

'Oh, I won't.' I smile at Patrick. 'I've built the company from the ground up, I feel very protective over it.'

Jack adds, 'Alicia has done a grand job. She's making a tidy profit on flexible hours. I'm very proud of her.'

Patrick coughs. 'Well, that's good to hear. But if you want to really grow and outstrip your competitors—'

'Then she knows exactly who to come to,' Jack quips.

Everyone laughs.

'Flexible work is a good thing too,' Dawn interjects. 'You'll need it when you and Jack start having a brood of your own.'

I try not to let the baby hints bring my mood down. I'm sure Dawn's words are kindly meant. So I push the thought from my mind and enjoy the Irish breakfast.

We carry on eating and chatting and, by the end of the meal, I'm feeling full and happy. I have everything I've ever wanted now. I'm Jack's wife and the sky's the limit from here. That's why I'm so intent on making this time with Jack's family go well.

I just need to make sure that I don't screw anything else up...

Chapter Twenty-Two

Jack

The time today seems to have rolled around quickly and Christmas Eve is upon us. We've had a quiet day as the continuation of the snow has meant that we've been stuck inside once more. We've all been engaging in simple, untaxing activities. Dawn has mostly been reading and gossiping on her phone with friends. Zara has sat transfixed in front of the TV, not saying much to anyone. I don't really know why she comes on these Christmas holidays. She gives off the air of really not wanting to be here and she's never fully embraced being a member of the Silver family. Ronan and my father did some crossword puzzles this morning, followed by some very competitive games of chess. It doesn't escape my notice that the pair of them seem to be joined at the hip.

I've always felt like a third wheel where my father and my brother are concerned. They're so alike, they have so much in common and they just seem to click. I've tried so hard to gain my father's approval but, no matter what I do, it never seems enough. My father's expectations are always so high and his disappointment regarding me has always been very apparent. He expected me to follow in his footsteps and to build my own business, to be an entrepreneur just like him. Except, he failed to teach me how to succeed in taking that path. He was so busy with work calls and going to the office when I was growing up that it's no wonder I had a closer relationship with my mother. I had no natural aptitude for creating something unique and profitable. So I went down another route instead. I'm good at what I do, I'm successful and one of the youngest members of the board of directors in my company's history. But my father is always telling me to get out of the job and be my own boss. It's not something I want and there's even more pressure these days because Ronan has proven himself to be a self-starter. His property empire is booming and my father's pride in his second son's achievements is clear.

Yasmin has been pacing around the lodge somewhat. She allowed baby Lily to have a bit of time in front of the TV and has since been alternating between feeding her and trying to get the little girl to sleep. It all looks very exhausting and I've noticed that Ronan is very hands off with Lily.

I look at Alicia. Kids were never on my agenda but, now I'm married, I sometimes find myself wondering what having a child would be like. What would we name a boy or a girl? Would I be a good father? Would I be better than my own dad has been to me?

I've spent a lot of time curled up with Alicia in front of the roaring fire in the last couple of days. We've been watching movies in the lounge, with Zara sitting in the armchair opposite us. I've also been sampling different Irish beers, as the fridge is fully stocked with a variety, and I'm feeling relaxed. Alicia has been her usual self with me, despite our argument yesterday. As the day has gone on, I've felt confident that she can't have connected the dots and realised the truth behind me marrying her.

Although I did let her in on a little family secret last night. Given how nervous and jittery she has been, I needed to give her more context to the Silver family dynamics, as well as explaining why certain family members have been behaving so badly. I was worried at first that Alicia wouldn't understand and that she'd be unable to keep a lid on her feelings about the news I'd unveiled to her. But she seems to be calm and collected today. Hopefully her new understanding will give her a fresh perspective on her place in this family. And make her a little less anxious about this holiday.

Anyway, secrets can't stay secrets forever. In the next few days, with us all in such close proximity, and with so much alcohol in the lodge, I'm pretty sure that things are going to unravel. And I, for one, can't wait to see it all play out. Because there's more than one person under this roof who's hiding something.

'Who's up for a family game night?' Dawn bustles into the lounge, an apron over her latest fluffy jumper.

Zara immediately sighs with scorn but Alicia is eager and nodding enthusiastically at the idea.

'I'll add that we've got Irish cheeses and crackers, followed by Guinness chocolate puddings to tempt you.'

'Go on then, count me in!' I say, my mouth watering at the thought of the Guinness chocolate puddings.

Dawn presents herself as an excellent cook, but, like most things in this family, this is only a facade. Admittedly, she has perfected pancakes and Irish breakfasts but, other than that, she's just very good at putting things in the oven and getting the timings right. The majority of meals she serves up, along with the delicious desserts that are rolled out during this holiday period, are all from a clever company that pre-makes home-cooked food and then allows canny housewives to pass them off as their own. Dawn has got a freezer full of these meals. I don't think Alicia has worked this out yet, but the rest of us are, of course, in the know. Dawn's kitchen prowess often features in our family banter after we've all had a few, much to Dawn's annoyance. But she still manages to pass off her pre-bought creations to an astonishing number of friends. It is just yet one more of the Silver family deceptions.

Alicia, Zara and I troop through to the kitchen. There are generous tumblers of Baileys waiting for us on the breakfast bar. I take a sip of mine. Nothing beats the creamy taste of Baileys.

'Right then,' Ronan says, a grin on his face. 'We thought first up would be Monopoly.'

We all groan collectively. Monopoly is a game that invariably ends in tears and yet we still end up playing it every year. Dad always wants to be the banker, Yasmin gets stroppy if anyone dares to try to buy any of the train stations out from under her, and Ronan gets cross if he doesn't get his mitts on Park Lane within the first couple of turns. As for me, I always have to be the boot. Don't ask me why, it's just the little silver piece that calls to me the most.

I glance at Alicia. This is perhaps not the best game to indoctrinate my wife into family games night with. She is completely unaware of all of these unwritten rules and is bound to take someone's preferred spot on the board without knowing the feelings this will invoke.

'Not yet!' Yasmin exclaims. 'I'm just taking Lily up to bed. No one set up Monopoly until I'm back down.'

Yasmin's face is deadly serious. She's usually in the final two when it comes to our Monopoly tournaments. She's highly competitive and completely ruthless when it comes to board games. She's definitely in it to win it.

'Okay, noted,' laughs Ronan.

'Let's do a simple game of charades first then,' I suggest, hoping this will be a good icebreaker.

'Oooh, what a good idea! I love charades,' exclaims Dawn.

'Say goodnight to everyone then,' Yasmin says to Lily, waving her little hand at us.

We all wave back or blow kisses before Yasmin whisks the baby upstairs, to the land of sleep.

'Let the games commence!' my father says, clapping his hands together and looking gleeful.

'I'll go first,' I volunteer, keen to put myself out there before Alicia gets pushed forward into the spotlight. I stand under the lights in the kitchen, gesticulating with my hands, trying to start the proceedings off with something easily guessable. Except, it's been a while and I end up flapping my arms about and looking ridiculous for far longer than I intended.

Five minutes in and everyone other than Zara is shouting suggestions, none of them remotely near to the film I'm trying to portray.

'Oh, how is no one else getting this, it's *Up*!' Zara eventually calls out.

'Yes! Yes, it is!' I'm genuinely excited that someone has finally got it. 'Your turn.'

Zara shrugs her shoulders. 'Really?'

'Yes, really, the winner takes the next turn, that's the rule.'

'Ugh, I best have another one of these then.' Zara pours another large helping of Baileys and downs it in one swift movement. She then takes my place and does a very straightforward job of communicating, 'I Want to Hold Your Hand', by The Beatles, which my father instantly guesses. He takes his turn and manages to bungle through, 'The Rose of Tralee'. His amateur dramatics gets everyone up and shouting out suggestions – even Zara this time. After a good few minutes, Alicia is the one to answer correctly. She looks shy but pleased that she's getting a chance to get involved.

My wife takes her place at the centre of the kitchen and I hold my breath, wondering how this will go. But Alicia does an absolutely hilarious job of acting out *March of the Penguins*, which ends with Dawn in stitches and my father belly-laughing. We keep going, each switching places and getting into more of a rhythm with guessing each other's line of thinking. It's good fun and we only break off when Yasmin re-joins the group.

'Ah, you missed out on some good craic there, Yas!' Ronan is wiping his eyes after watching Dawn mime *Pirates of the Caribbean*.

'Yep, nice one!' I nod in agreement.

'See, who needs technology to entertain them. This is what we used to do in the good old days,' Dawn says, flushed from laughter and looking misty-eyed with nostalgia.

Everyone has had at least a couple of generous proportions of Baileys by this point.

'Let's have the cheese and crackers now,' Dawn suggests. She begins dishing out assorted crackers, chutneys, piccalilli and some of Ireland's finest cheeses. It looks like Dawn has had a great old time at a Christmas market or two, judging by the selection she has on offer. Alongside the cheeseboard options, there are a number of dips, grapes, sliced meats and vegetable crudités. There's not quite enough fruit and veg to balance out the sheer amount of dairy that's now dominating the table, but I'm very much okay with that.

As we're working our way through cheese and wine, I manage to give Alicia a quick heads-up on everyone's Monopoly preferences and my wife seems to appreciate getting the low-down ahead of the game. I am trying to give her a bit more guidance, but I'm still very new in my role as someone's husband.

I eat far too much and I'm left feeling like I'm going to need a crane to yank me up from my seat. But it's Christmas, and if you can't overindulge at Christmastime, when can you?

As the evening passes, our group chats amiably. The wine and the Baileys has gone down very well and the atmosphere is more chilled than it has been. The undercurrent of tension seems to have dissolved for now – or maybe I'm just a bit drunk.

'Let's get going on the main event then,' Yasmin says, laying out the Monopoly board.

'Boot please!' I pipe up.

'As if I could forget.' Yasmin gives me a knowing grin.

'Where is the top hat?' My father's sausage-like fingers are riffling through the little velvet bag containing all of the Monopoly pieces.

'Don't sweat, it's here,' Yasmin replies, placing the silver figure in front of him.

'You better nab a piece now,' Dawn jokes to Alicia.

'Oh, I don't mind.'

'What do you usually go for?'

'I haven't played Monopoly since I was a child, so I honestly don't mind.'

'Well, you're in for the game of your life then,' my father promises.

It's good to see him warming to Alicia. It's important to me that he likes her.

We all settle down at the table, strategies being turned over in alcohol-soaked minds. The dice is rolled and the first few rounds are played in earnest. I can see the determined look in Yasmin's eyes and the sharp expression on my father's face. For someone who hasn't played the game for a long time, Alicia is doing well. She's certainly giving Ronan and Yasmin a run for their money.

'Excuse me,' my father says abruptly. He looks a little pale as he slides his chair back from the table.

'Are you okay?' Dawn asks, concern written across her features.

My father nods shakily and then heads for the door.

A good few minutes pass and then Dawn also absents herself from the game and follows my father.

'Let's have a break here. I want to make sure I'm thrashing everyone fair and square,' Yasmin says through a mouthful of crackers.

'Drink?' I enquire, to which I'm met with lots of affirmatives.

I grab a fresh bottle of red wine and make sure everyone is topped up.

'Is your dad okay?' Alicia asks me quietly.

'I think so...' I trail off. He did look quite pale all of a sudden. 'I need the loo, so I'll go and check on him.'

'Everyone's dropping like flies,' I hear Ronan say as I too disappear out of the kitchen door.

I make my way to the downstairs bathroom. There's no sign of Dawn or my father in the lounge or the small office at the front of the lodge. So I creep silently up the stairs and pause halfway up. I can hear low voices – it sounds like they're on the other side of the main bathroom, which is directly next to the top of the staircase.

I go up a few more steps and the conversation becomes a little clearer. The door to the bathroom must be slightly ajar, but I can't quite see. I strain my ears and pick up snippets of dialogue. I slowly start to put together the phrases and then it clicks. I know exactly what they're talking about.

My heart speeds up and my mouth is dry.

I finally have the answer to a question that's been bothering me for a long time.

And confirmation the risky plan I have set in motion is working.

Now it's really time to let the games begin...

Chapter Twenty-Three

Yasmin

'Is your internet connecting?' Zara queries, glaring down at the glow of her phone screen.

'Yeah, I'm sure mine is.' Alicia picks up her phone from where it was resting at the side of the Monopoly board and checks it. 'Oh, no. Mine's gone too.'

'Me three,' chimes in Ronan. 'Zero bars of connectivity.'

'You're joking me,' Zara moans. 'I hope this isn't going to last for long.'

I give Ronan a furtive look and Zara catches it.

'What? What does that look mean?' Zara blurts out.

Spending time with Zara is often uncomfortable because she's so straight-talking. She doesn't bother to dress up her words or even try to sound a little bit more polite.

'It means this has happened before,' Ronan tells her honestly.

'And?' Zara's voice is laced with impatience. Everything about her grates on me.

'And... it took a while before normal service resumed.'

Zara is looking at Ronan like he severed access to the internet. As though it's my husband's fault that the bad weather is interfering with our connectivity. 'A while as in minutes or hours?'

'As in days.'

'Days?! Seriously?'

'Calm down, Zara,' I snap. I've had enough of her abrasiveness. I don't know how she gets away with it all the time. Dawn never calls her out on her behaviour and, somehow, even Patrick lets it slide. 'We're in a remote part of Ireland. The internet connection can be a bit patchy here on a good day, let alone in the middle of winter. We've been lucky with it so far.'

Zara shakes her head, her exasperation coming off her in waves. She mutters something under her breath.

'What did you just say?' I lean forward, my face stern.

'Nothing,' Zara snaps back at me.

I'm almost certain I heard her say that she wished she'd never come on the holiday. I hope that's the case and that she never comes on another trip to Ireland. She is resentful and disdainful with all of us. Her presence drags down the mood when she does join in with the group. And the rest of the time she sulks upstairs in her room. Why does Dawn never have a word with her about it? I wouldn't allow my own daughter to behave in that way.

I cross my fingers and pray that she won't be joining us again on next year's Christmas trip.

The minutes tick by and Patrick, Dawn and Jack are still out of the room.

'I'm going to cut some malt loaf, does anyone else want some?'

I didn't eat a lot of the cheese and crackers because I rarely eat dairy these days. And I only ever eat malt loaf when I'm here at the lodge on this annual Christmas holiday, a once-a-year treat. It's the perfect mix between savoury and sweet, the treacle and raisins combined with the chewy, stodgy goodness.

Zara comes over to the kitchen area. 'I'll have some.' Her voice is even – I can't tell if she's still in a strop or if she's got over her strop about the internet already.

I take a knife from the block and start slicing.

Ronan is over on the far side of the kitchen, fumbling around with something, and then he says, 'Er, hate to break it to you, but the landline has gone as well.'

'Oh, what! This place really is out in the sticks!' Zara lets rip with her annoyance once more, yanking open the cutlery draw and snatching up some forks.

'Look,' I snarl at her, 'just stop whining. If Patrick comes back in and you're griping about the internet and the phone, it's going to end in another terrible evening.'

Zara's face blanches and it is only then I realise I still have the knife in my hand. Zara's body is just inches from the tip of the sharp blade and she looks more than a little afraid.

I allow the steel knife to hover for just a second longer than I should and then I let it clatter onto the shiny, kitchen worktop.

Zara quickly retreats back to the table and I resume my task of plating up the malt bread before handing it out.

Minutes later, Jack slips back into his seat and, not long after, Dawn and Patrick are back in the room too. Patrick seems subdued and I'm guessing that he and Dawn have had words over something.

The game of Monopoly resumes and quickly picks up pace. Now Lily is in bed, it's my time to shine. To show everyone how quick-thinking I still am and that I've still got it when it comes to banter. Jack is sitting beside me and we end up laughing and talking together in a way that we haven't done for a long time. Not since he proposed to Alicia.

One by one, people begin to fall out of the game. First Dawn, then Zara, then Jack. I'm impressed by some of Alicia's moves – she's more strategic than I thought she was going to be. I manage to outmanoeuvre my husband and he goes crashing out of the game when I bankrupt him. Unfortunately, Ronan's lack of grip over his finances mirrors reality and I think this hits home for him too as he moodily announces that he's off to bed.

I don't let my husband distract me, though. I'm playing to win. It's me up against Patrick and Alicia. To my surprise, Patrick is knocked out of the game next. He usually puts up more of a fight. So it's just down to me and my new sister-in-law.

The thrill of being neck and neck with someone, almost at the finish line, spurs me on. All the more so because it's my real-life rival. I love playing games like this because after all, isn't that life? It's all a game really. We're all just working out what our next move is going to be. We all want to be winners. But there have to be some losers too.

I've been on a winning streak ever since I married Ronan. But things have been slipping through my fingers lately. My winning dice rolls aren't so frequent anymore. I need to sharpen my focus and make sure that I'm upping my game. It's true that I've been dealt some good hands in my time, especially since I've been Yasmin Silver. But my younger years also taught me how to play a poor hand well too.

Finally, in one deft move, I manage to clear Alicia out of money. Those remaining at the table give me a round of applause and Alicia gives me a gracious shake of the hand.

I've won. I've kept my crown as the Queen of Monopoly.
And I plan to keep on winning at the game of life too.

Chapter Twenty-Four

Alicia

Christmas Eve morning rolls around, but no one is up quite so early today. Patrick announced before the end of yesterday evening that he was going to have a lie-in this morning. Jack told me when we went up to bed that his father having a lie-in was practically unheard of. I'm just pleased to not be up at first light again. Even though yesterday we mostly lounged about, we've been up past midnight every night. I like to have a solid eight hours of sleep, otherwise my head feels as though it's been stuffed with cotton wool and I can't function properly.

This morning's breakfast offering is potato cakes with salmon and cream cheese. I was so impressed with the array of authentic Irish food that has been served up, but Jack told me the majority of what we've consumed has not been made by Dawn's fair hands. The meals have come from a high-end home-cooked meal company. I was astonished to discover the food was basically posh ready meals, but I've enjoyed eating it all the same.

As soon as we've eaten and cleared away, everyone has paired off to do their own thing again. As much as I've enjoyed watching festive films in front of the warming fire, I'm feeling a bit caged up and antsy today. I tend to go out running every morning and I feel a bit out of sorts because I don't have my usual routine in place. So I decide that before I slump down onto the squashy sofa, I'm going to do something productive.

'What do you want to do then?' Jack teases, laughing at me for already being bored of relaxing.

'Um, how about some yoga?' I suggest.

'No, I ate way too much cheese last night.'

'That's the point.'

Jack holds his stomach. 'Maybe later, the thought of bending over my cheese baby right now makes me feel ill.'

'How about teaching me to play chess?'

Jack leans in close and whispers to me, 'I don't really understand the rules.'

I snort with amusement. I wasn't expecting him to say this, but now I understand why he wasn't engaging in the chess tournament with Patrick and Ronan yesterday.

'Maybe we should get Patrick or Ronan to teach us both then?'

Jack shakes his head. 'That's my idea of hell.'

'Fair enough.'

'Let's just watch TV,' Jack wheedles.

'No, I want to make memories.'

'We can make memories in front of the TV.'

'Okay, you go and chill out until the cheese is out of your system and I'll find something to do.'

'Are you sure?' Jack questions. 'The cheese may still be running through my bloodstream until next week.'

I laugh at the silly face my husband is pulling. 'Go,' I shoo him out of my way. He gives me a lingering kiss and then slopes off into the lounge. Zara has already bagged a spot in her favourite armchair and I'm guessing she is set for the next few hours as well.

I head into the kitchen and open the fridge. Noting the ingredients available, I decide to make some cupcakes. Yes, we've probably got enough food to last us weeks, but I rarely get the chance to cook and I want to show off my red velvet cupcake recipe. Patrick let slip the other day that red velvet is his favourite type of cake, so I also want to make the cupcakes to help build bridges with my father-in-law.

I check through the cupboards in the vast kitchen and eventually locate everything I need. I check my phone; the internet still isn't working, so I bring up a playlist that I have saved and fill my workspace with music. I pull on an apron and get started. There's something about baking that gives me a warm glow. I think it's because I spent many happy hours baking with my mother when I was a child.

Yasmin comes into the kitchen with Lily on her hip.

'Hi,' I say to them both. 'I'm making red velvet cupcakes.'

Lily's face seems to light up at the mention of cake.

'I'm putting beetroot in the mix, is that okay for Lily?' I ask Yasmin.

She nods in response and transfers Lily to her other hip. Lily is stretching out a chubby hand for my wooden spoon.

'Will she be okay with the other ingredients?' I gesture to the various packets scattered across the worktop.

Yasmin pulls another wooden spoon out of a kitchen draw and hands it to her little girl, who's now babbling away. 'Um, yeah that should all be fine. She'll either eat it or she won't, you never know with kids.'

Yasmin disappears again and I'm left on my own.

It doesn't take too long to make the cupcakes. They're looking good and, as I pop them in the oven, I'm confident that I'm going to get a good rise on them. Washing the worktop and then my hands, I set the timer on the oven and hang up the apron which has remained pristine throughout my stint in the kitchen.

I'm now ready to surrender myself to a few hours of checking out in front of the TV, safe in the knowledge that I've achieved something today and hopefully my good deed will work towards improving the relationship with my in-laws.

**

'These are delicious!' The red velvet cupcakes are freshly iced and Patrick has already devoured one of them. 'I might just have to have one more.' He reaches for another cupcake.

I beam with joy. This was exactly the reaction I was hoping for. My recipe has been tried, tested and perfected over the years. I've made it many times and I think this might just be my best batch yet.

We're all gathered in the elegant kitchen once again. We've just had a lunch of traditional Irish stew and the cupcakes were the perfect thing to round off the meal.

'Mmm, they're good!' Compliments from Zara seem like a rarity, so I take this as a win.

'Nice work!' my husband says, licking his lips. 'You'll have to make these a regular occurrence at home.'

'They are divine,' Yasmin adds.

Yes! I think to myself. I've finally won my sister-in-law over.

'Can you give me the recipe?' she asks.

'Of course,' I chirp happily. 'It was my mum's recipe, but I've tweaked and changed it over the years.'

Yasmin nods thoughtfully. 'There's a hint of something that I can't quite put my finger on.'

'Lemon?' I supply.

'No, it's not the lemon. Although the subtle hint of citrus is a nice touch. It's something else.' Yasmin takes another bite and ponders for a bit.

'What ingredients have you used?' Jack asks, taking a sip of his freshly brewed coffee.

'Eggs, butter, sugar, lemon...' I reel the list of ingredients off by heart. 'There's some beetroot in there.' Seeing the beetroot in the fridge was actually what gave me the idea to make the red velvet cupcakes in the first place. It's a great natural ingredient and means you don't have to use red food colouring. 'Flour, of course... oh, and my secret ingredient.'

I pause for effect.

'I use half flour and half ground almonds. The almonds give such a great texture.'

'Beetroot in cake, I would never have guessed!' grins Ronan. 'It tastes good.'

'Almonds?' Zara queries.

'Yeah, there wasn't quite enough flour in the cupboard, so I just topped up with the ground almonds for the quantity needed.'

'What!' Patrick is on his feet and looks suddenly enraged.

My heart plummets. Oh no, what have I done now?

'You put almonds in there?' Dawn follows up quietly.

'Yes...'

'Dawn is allergic to nuts!' Patrick fumes.

'Oh my God, I didn't know!' I exclaim. No one had told me that Dawn had a nut allergy. 'I'm so sorry, Dawn, I didn't realise.' This is such a disaster.

Patrick has turned puce by this point.

'It's okay,' Dawn states unconvincingly. 'At least we know about it now, so I can deal with it as quickly as possible. 'Zara, could you grab me an antihistamine?'

'An antihistamine? Don't you want your EpiPen? After what happened last time?' Yasmin offers, before Zara can answer.

Dawn's face falls at this remark. 'Yes, on second thoughts best use the EpiPen. It's in my handbag in my room.'

Yasmin swiftly exits the room.

'Is there anything I can do?' My stomach feels hollow. I can't believe I've messed up again.

'No, no. Don't worry.' I notice a small red rash beginning to flare up on Dawn's hand.

I feel nauseous. What a colossal mistake to make.

Yasmin rushes back in and hands the EpiPen to Dawn. Patrick continues to glare at me. I wanted to do something that would win the favour of my in-laws but instead I've just made things much worse.

Dawn fumbles with the case of the EpiPen, her left hand is suddenly a glowing red. The reaction has come on quickly, so she must have quite a strong allergic reaction to nuts. Why did no one tell me this?

'Alicia, you didn't know,' Yasmin says, her eyes narrowed as she's looking at me.

Except, now the first wave of panic has passed, I realise I had checked the ingredients with Yasmin when she came into the kitchen. I asked her if Lily was okay with beetroot, as I know some people can have reactions to that, and Yasmin also said Lily would be fine with the rest of the ingredients. She didn't mention anything about nuts being an issue for Dawn. Everything was out on the kitchen worktop. Surely, Yasmin saw the packet of ground almonds there as well?

It also strikes me as odd that there would even be a bag of ground almonds in the cupboard if Dawn has a severe allergy to nuts. But then I remember that Dawn and Patrick only use the lodge a few times a year, whereas Ronan and Yasmin use the place several times a month. So I guess the ground almonds must belong to Yasmin. I can feel the frustration bubbling inside me. Has my sister-in-law set me up again?

I open my mouth to protest, but Yasmin scoops up Lily, cooing, 'Nap time,' to her daughter. She whisks Lily out of the room, leaving the rest of us to deal with the fallout of Dawn's reaction. Patrick now has an arm around Dawn and Zara is handing her stepmother a glass of water. Jack is frowning at me, with a look in his eyes that I don't like.

Did my sister-in-law deliberately withhold information? Or was she just distracted?

Chapter Twenty-Five

Now

I'm sitting in the high-backed chair, my whole body trembling with cold and with fear. I've been marched into the little office at the front of the lodge and I've been sat here, unable to move, for at least fifteen minutes.

Two of the Garda officers are planted in front of the door, my only exit route, as if there's a risk that I might jump up and try to run back out into the sub-zero conditions.

This has to be a mistake. A nightmare that will quickly be put right.

The police found me out in the snow, just metres away from the gruesome body on the ground. It was a case of the wrong time, and the wrong place. I was outside as part of the search party. I was trying to help. And now look where that's got me.

I'm cursing my choice to come on this holiday. I could've said no. I could've stayed at home and not had to deal with interacting with the Silver family or getting caught up in their twisted family dynamics...

After what seems like hours, I hear a commotion outside the room I'm in. Someone is shouting, but I can't make out who. And lots of voices are fighting with each other to take control of whatever argument is happening.

'What's going on?'

Neither of the officers answer me.

Things go quiet. I'm left to my own thoughts circling round and round.

I have to make them understand that I played no part in the murder of the poor person out in the snow.

A more senior officer barges into the office, the door banging loudly behind him.

'Mrs Silver?' the gruff voice asks.

'Yes,' I croak out my reply.

'I've got some questions for you.'

Chapter Twenty-Six

Yasmin

'Toy!' Lily's face is a picture. With some help from Ronan, she's just ripped open the bright red wrapping paper and discovered her first Christmas gift inside. She squeals in delight at the big pink pig and cuddles it tightly. I snap a photograph. Lily's first Christmas morning is a special milestone and I want to make sure that I capture as much of it as possible.

I automatically go to upload the photo to Instagram, but then I remember that I can't because the Wi-Fi is still down. I sigh. As much as I berated Zara about her grumpiness over the lack of internet signal, it is a pain. We're so used to being able to ping a message to a friend, quickly Google the answer to something or connect with a wide network of people across social media platforms. Not having access to phone signal or the internet is making this whole snowed-in experience a lot more intense. Without the option to escape from the current situation with a few minutes of social media scrolling or the ability to gossip with one of my friends via instant messaging, things feel a lot more claustrophobic. The days seem to be dragging on and, even though it was only the night before last that we lost access to the outside world, it seems a lot longer.

The lodge stands in a remote part of the Wicklow Mountains; there aren't any other buildings for a good few miles. A cluster of old cottages forms part of a boutique holiday resort, about six or seven miles away, but we don't have any close neighbours nearby. This, I'm sure, was part of the appeal for Patrick when he first purchased the lodge many years ago, before his sons left home. In the summertime, it is glorious. There's acres of space to enjoy and I can't wait for Lily to be able to learn to ride a bike up here or climb a tree in the woodland area just down the hill.

Ronan and I have been using the place regularly in recent summers. There are enough rooms in the lodge that we can invite friends and have a proper weekend getaway. But the winter is a different matter. It feels so isolated up here. We've never had the weather quite this bad before either and cabin fever is definitely starting to set in. I hope the snow begins to thaw soon.

'More!' Lily claps her hands and reaches for a small, square-shaped present that Patrick is handing to her. He lifts Lily up onto his knee and they unwrap the brightly coloured package together. Patrick looks happier today. Yesterday, his black mood hung over the occupants of the lodge like a large looming cloud. He was understandably not impressed with Alicia giving Dawn an allergic reaction.

I stifle a laugh at the thought of it. Alicia looked so bewildered. And Patrick was so mad, he ended up binning the rest of the cupcakes, which was a shame as they were actually quite scrummy. But it was Alicia's fault for not checking to see if anyone had allergies. She asked me if Lily was okay with beetroot and the other ingredients, but she should have made sure that everyone else was okay to eat the cupcakes as well. She will certainly have learnt her lesson. It's so important to do your research when you join a new family. Alicia so far is showing that she really hasn't invested enough time and energy in sussing everyone out.

Alicia is still very subdued. She's sitting with Jack on the other side of the expansive Christmas tree. The fairy lights are twinkling on the branches and there's a mountain of parcels underneath it. The scene looks so festive. Everyone is decked out in their Christmas outfits. The men have seasonal jumpers on, complete with merry slogans. I'm wearing a long, red cable-knit woollen dress that I know Ronan is keen on. Alicia has her hair in a pretty French plait. She's wearing sparkly silver tights and a short black skirt and mid-rise top, along with a chunky black cardigan. I raise my eyebrow as I realise that Zara's style must be rubbing off on Alicia. Or maybe Alicia deliberately chose her mostly black ensemble because she thought Zara would approve? Zara is sitting on the other side of the room. She is wearing dark, ripped jeans, an oversized black jumper and her look is topped off with silver rings adorning each of her fingers, along with a number of silver hoops in her earlobes. She looks the least festive of us all.

Dawn is still upstairs in bed. She had terrible hives and stomach cramps last night, despite the early intervention of the EpiPen. She has promised that she will be downstairs soon, but when I checked in on her this morning, she clearly wasn't feeling well. This, of course, means that I'll need to step up with the food preparations today. I've made sure the turkey is in the oven along with the vegetables. Patrick and Dawn have already both praised me for swooping in and sorting out the meal. I was planning on helping out with Christmas lunch anyway, but now I'll be able to claim all the praise for the festive roast. Although, in typical Dawn style, a lot of the food was from her pre-made meal source so there actually wasn't a lot of work involved in pulling everything together. All in all, this has been another win for me.

Ronan hands me a gift. It's a small, square box. I unwrap it slowly, enjoying the anticipation, and then exclaim when I open it. An exquisite white gold locket is lying on a velvet cushion. I open it up and find a picture of Lily inside. It's the perfect gift. I've trained my husband well.

I smile up at him. 'Thank you, Ronan, it's beautiful.'

'Phew!' Ronan dramatically swipes his hand across his brow in mock exaggeration.

I give him a peck on the cheek and then hand him a silver envelope. Ronan has so many things that he's hard to buy for. So for his main present this year, I've gone for concert tickets for his favourite band.

'Wow! This is incredible!' Ronan punches the air. 'How did you manage to get tickets? I thought they all sold out within minutes?

I tap my nose. 'That's for me to know.'

My husband folds me into an embrace. I thought the tickets would go down a storm. I'm glad he's happy with them.

Patrick and Lily are opening another gift. We're slowly working our way through them. Lily has been thoroughly spoiled. The majority of parcels under the shimmering tree are for her. Patrick has gone to town for his first grandchild's first Christmas and Lily is unwrapping all sorts of wonderful presents. From cute slippers to a rocking horse, Lily is one lucky little girl.

I open a few more presents myself. My husband has sweetly given me a stocking filled with all of my favourite pamper and beauty items. I now have enough moisturisers and make-up to get me through the first six months of the year. I also receive a Jo Malone candle from Zara, which is much better than her gifts from previous years, and a new Mulberry purse from Alicia and Jack.

My husband is chuffed to bits with a posh cocktail making set that his brother has given to him. And Lily is thoroughly entertained with the crunching and scrunching of all of the colourful wrapping paper that's strewn across the floor.

I overhear Alicia apologising to Zara for not getting her a gift, but Zara doesn't seem to mind.

I swear that Christmas Day is the longest day ever. I enjoy it to a degree, but it always feels endless. This year, Lily's reaction is definitely making the morning feel more fun and I continue to snap photographs of her, crawling in the wrapping and exploring her new toys. I make sure to keep her at the opposite end of the room to the Christmas tree. She keeps looking over at it longingly but I'm keen not to repeat the broken bauble incident of the other day, particularly now Dawn is feeling even more fragile.

Eventually, Dawn does join our group. She looks a lot better than she did yesterday but still not quite right. She perks up a little bit when Patrick hands her a gift bag to open. Dawn pulls out a gorgeous little snow globe. Inside it is a photograph of her and Patrick standing in front of Bartley Lodge. She shakes the globe and watches the snow fall. Patrick usually lavishes Dawn with expensive perfumes and jewellery. This gift is more personal and completely out of the ordinary for him.

Dawn's grey eyes fill with tears. 'Thank you, it's gorgeous.' She sniffs and shakes the globe again. Patrick is now looking misty-eyed too.

'I wanted you to have this as a memento of our Christmases together,' he says to his wife before reaching out for her hand. 'I wanted you to have something to remind you of me every Christmas Day from now on.'

'Oh Patrick, don't talk like that.' She's clutching his hand hard now and the tears begin to flow down her cheeks.

'We'll have plenty of Christmases left together. You'll see.'

Patrick shakes his head. 'But we might not. We've got to face facts. I want you to remember the good times we've had together.'

'We have had some good times, haven't we?' Dawn sniffs again and then places the snow globe back in the bag.

I'm holding my breath, waiting to hear what Patrick says next. He puts an arm around Dawn, who is wiping her tears away with the back of her hand.

The elephant in the room has finally been spoken of.

'Look, kids,' Patrick says, casting an eye over each of us in turn. 'Things might have got off to a rocky start this holiday,' he pauses and rubs his forehead. 'I... I just wanted to say thank you all for coming here this year. I don't say this often, but it does mean a lot.'

'Dad, we all want to be here,' Ronan says emphatically.

'Is there something wrong? Have you had your results back?' Jack questions, leaning forward in his chair.

This is the undercurrent that has been bubbling underneath every interaction. It's no wonder that Patrick has been so emotional and moody over the last few days. He was told in early November that he had cancer. The treatment under his private health care started almost immediately. He has a week's pause over Christmas, but the question of how well he responds to medical intervention is a big cloud hanging over him – and over all of us.

'No, the results aren't back until January,' Patrick says gruffly. 'Whatever they are, I want to make sure we all have an excellent Christmas here together.'

'And we will do. The very best.' I make sure that my voice is clear and reassuring. I want Patrick to view me as a steady presence, someone he can rely on to keep things on an even keel whilst everything is up in the air.

'Yes, let's make this one unforgettable.' Patrick responds with a watery smile.

I smile because I'm going to make sure this is a Christmas that all of us will remember...

Chapter Twenty-Seven

Jack

My father has finally come out and said something. I feel like I've been tiptoeing round the issue of his diagnosis since I first arrived at the lodge. I have no idea what to say or do in this situation. My father is such a proud man that it's hard to know how to give him support. It's clear that he doesn't want anyone's sympathy or to be viewed any differently to his usual self. I completely get that. I think I'd be the same. But everyone handles situations like this differently. When you're faced with a health prognosis such as this, it puts mortality into a very stark light.

My father called me in November to let me know about his cancer diagnosis. I was stunned. He has this air of indestructibility about him. I didn't see a bill of ill health on the horizon for him. Yet here it is.

After my initial shock at my father's news, I made sure to ring him more often than I usually do and to check in for updates on what was going on with his treatment. He has been very practical about the whole thing. And, ever pragmatic, he didn't really want to discuss it until he knew the results of his treatment. He has given little away over the last few weeks, so I'm not sure how he has reacted to his current treatment or what the doctors have said to him in terms of his chances of beating this cancer. It's amazing what can be done these days, if things are caught at the right time, and I'm inclined to be optimistic about his survival rate. If he was ten years older I might be more worried but he's fit as an Irish fiddle and I'm certain he will fight this with everything he has.

This is the secret I told my wife the other night. She was saddened by the news, but it helped her to understand why Patrick flew off the handle when Nuala was locked outside. This is only one of the many family secrets hiding just under the surface of the perfect image we all present but she'll find out more soon enough.

As we all continue on with the day, opening up our last presents, my father looks as though there's a weight off his shoulders. Perhaps speaking to us all together has allowed him to share his thoughts and therefore shed the load on his mind. I recall the whispered exchange that I heard the other night between my father and Dawn.

'The doctor will be in touch with more news next week.' My father's voice was a low rumble.

'Patrick, I think you're going to need to take it a bit easier than usual. All these late nights can't be doing you any good.'

There was a pause.

'Promise me? You need to let me look after you.'

I didn't hear my father's response – he was talking too quietly for me to make it out. But there was something else that I overheard. Something that I had been anxious to find out more about. Dawn mentioned going to a solicitor's office in January, after my father receives his results. I was intrigued by this part of their exchange.

'Yes, I'll go to see them as soon as I've had the results,' was my father's reply. 'I want to make sure all of my affairs are in order.'

I thought my father would be making plans for his estate, and potentially his retirement, given his current circumstances. Since overhearing snippets of their conversation, I can't help but wonder what he wants to discuss with his solicitor. As well as his vast business empire, my father owns this lodge, a large townhouse in central Dublin and he has a well-positioned flat in London too. That's not to mention the stocks and shares that he has to his name. My father always said that he intended to split the majority of his worldly goods between me and Ronan. Marrying Dawn altered things, but my father indicated that he would leave her the flat in London along with a generous sum of money. Perhaps things have changed, though? And maybe Dawn, knowing her husband's health is hanging in the balance, is trying to ensure that his will is updated, to leave her with more assets.

It's something that has been bothering me ever since. I should really talk to Ronan about it, but I want to find out more myself. Because another conversation, one from almost a year ago, has also been playing on my mind. My father sat me down, just after our last Christmas stay at the lodge, and told me in no uncertain terms that if I didn't get married and start behaving in a more grown-up manner, then he would have no choice but to disinherit me – or at least dramatically reduce my share.

I was flabbergasted when he told me. I was still managing to hold down a high-profile job in the city, and I thought that my father at least respected that. After doing some digging, it turned out that a friend of a friend had told his parents about some of my more alternative, recreational ways of letting off steam and relaxing from the pressures of my job, as well as the wild parties I attended regularly. I was infuriated that this information had reached my father's ears, but there was nothing

I could do to change his mind. His messaging was non-negotiable. If I didn't find a wife and have a family then the majority of his money would go to my younger brother and his child.

I simmered and stewed on this from early January and into February. I didn't want to give up the life I loved. I also didn't want to give in to my father's pressures and demands. And yet, there was a lot at stake. I needed to do something to change my father's mind. I resented him trying to push me into making decisions that I wasn't ready for, and perhaps never would be.

I discussed the matter with a close friend and the solution quickly became clear. Alicia was the woman who had stuck by my side throughout our twenties. Even though I had never wanted a steady girlfriend, Alicia seemed happy to slot into my life in whatever way I wanted. She had never put any labels on our relationship and I trusted her. The only problem was, Alicia had gone travelling and I wasn't sure when she was returning to the UK. Around that time, she stopped replying to my messages in her usual eager way and took forever to get back to me. Her social media feeds showed her having the time of her life in Thailand. She was pictured frequently with a fair woman with a short blonde bob and in big groups of men and women, all with tousled hair, enviable tans and smiling faces.

Just when I needed Alicia the most, I thought I'd lost her. I'd never really given much thought to how I might feel if Alicia stepped back from my life. She had been such a constant presence for so many years that it wasn't even a question that had entered my mind. But she was gone precisely when I needed her the most.

I managed to extract from her when she was coming back to England and I made sure I was at the airport with a big bunch of flowers, waiting for her as she stepped off the plane. She came running straight into my arms.

After that, I wined and dined her for several weeks and then whisked her off to Paris to propose in a bigger way than my first attempt the night she returned from globetrotting. It was romantic and even I was swept up in the moment. But the real reason I was marrying Alicia wasn't for romance or love. It was because I didn't want to lose my inheritance. The inheritance that was due to me. My poor mother would turn in her grave if my father did follow through with his threats, but I knew what my father was like and he wouldn't think twice about cutting me out of his will. He divorced my mother because of her alcohol addiction and he was clearly appalled by my use of recreational drugs and prepared to cut me off as well. It was all I could do to stop him carting me off to rehab, which was completely ridiculous and unnecessary. I knew the only way to turn things around was to do what he'd asked.

Alicia and I planned our wedding quickly, with a date set for early autumn. We'd known each other for such a long time so there was no reason to wait. My father was pleased with the abrupt turn of events in my life. I thought that would put a stop to any notion of him changing my inheritance. But perhaps not if he plans on going to see his solicitor? Perhaps I was wrong and he is going to reduce my share of his estate anyway. Maybe my marriage this year was too little, too late? Maybe Alicia has made one mistake too many over the holiday...

I need to make sure he doesn't go to that solicitor's office and make unfavourable changes to his will. I need to come up with a plan to change his mind.

Because my future depends on it.

And it's not just my financial future hanging in the balance. There's much more at stake. I've made a few mistakes in my time but, in this last year, I've got myself into a situation that is far more perilous than I'd bargained for. So it's not just money at risk if I don't receive my full inheritance, my life is in danger too...

Chapter Twenty-Eight

Alicia

'It's a fine thing, to be surrounded by all of your family.' Patrick announces, as he holds his glass aloft.

'Give over, old fella,' Ronan heckles him.

'Don't worry, I'm not going to go overboard with another speech, I just wanted to make a little toast.'

Patrick raises his glass once more and says, 'To Christmas and to family.'

'To Christmas and to family.' We all echo his words and raise our glasses as well.

'You can all crack on with your food now.'

We all follow his suggestion eagerly as we pick up our knives and forks. It's another incredible spread. My plate is brimming with roast potatoes, stuffing, turkey and an assortment of roasted vegetables. I'm bound to have put on a few pounds by the end of this holiday, with the combination of tasty food and lazing about for most of the day. I'll have to get my running shoes on pronto when I get back to London in January.

I'm relieved that Patrick's illness is now out in the open. It was awkward knowing about it but not knowing if I should say anything. I was glad that Jack had entrusted me with the sad news but I was also worried about keeping my knowledge under wraps, because I'm not very good at keeping secrets.

'The Christmas crackers!' Dawn cries.

'Yes, we mustn't forget them,' Yasmin agrees. A clattering sound echoes around the table as we each abandon our cutlery.

I run the fingers on my right hand over my left arm. The skin just below my wrist is still stretched and sore after the incident with the candle a few evenings ago. At least there aren't any candles alight on this table.

'Just be careful today,' Ronan jokes. 'We don't want any more accidents Alicia.' His tone is jovial enough, but I inwardly cringe at the comment. I'm sure everyone was thinking the same thing but did he really need to highlight it?

'That will be a tale to tell in years to come.' Jack winks at me.

I can't think of anything to quip back at him, so I give him a small smile instead and pray that he's right.

We pull our Christmas crackers, without anyone getting hurt this time. Colourful paper hats are placed on the top of everyone's heads. Yasmin puts a crown on Lily and it slips down over her eyes. Patrick croons over his sweet granddaughter.

I'm starving by now but, before we all tuck in, everyone takes a turn at reading out their jokes. It's amazing how a little cardboard tube and some cheesy lines that everyone has heard a million times before can bring joy to the faces of each person around the table.

Ronan and Jack then descend into exchanging the most awful banter they can think of. For the first time, I get a glimpse of how the two men may have interacted as children or teenagers. They're all too keen to keep egging each other on, until Jack goes one step too far with a rather vulgar limerick.

'Enough!' Patrick commands, raising his voice over the now giggling grown-up men. 'We don't need that kind of language at the dinner table.'

There's a twinkle in Jack's eye as he turns away from his father's gaze to look at me, biting back a grin. I'm reminded of Jack's natural spontaneity. Amongst our group of friends, he is invariably the prankster. He's the person who arrives first on a night out and leaves last. That was part of the draw for me, Jack helps to bring me out of my shell and when I'm with him, I find myself enjoying life more.

As the laughter comes to an end, we all get down to the business of eating. The food is absolutely to die for. The roast potatoes have the perfect hint of rosemary, the carrots are honey-glazed and the gravy is just the right thickness. A contented silence settles over the Silver family as we all enjoy our festive feast.

'This is amazing!' I direct my compliment at Yasmin. There's been frostiness from her, I still don't know why, and she's done some awful things to me. But this is my olive branch.

'You've done a stellar job, Yas,' Ronan agrees.

'Thanks so much for stepping in at the eleventh hour,' Dawn chimes in.

I feel super uncomfortable at this, as we all know why Dawn was unable to cook the Christmas dinner as planned. I tried to assist Yasmin, but she practically shooed me out of the kitchen. I guess after my baking disaster, she didn't trust me to go near a roast dinner.

'It's a Christmas miracle that you pulled it together,' Jack adds.

I detect a note of sarcasm in my husband's voice. I look around the table. It seems no one else has picked up on it, but it was definitely there. I try to ignore the niggling feeling that Jack is deliberately antagonising Yasmin and focus on eating my food.

I think back to Christmases with my own parents. It was always a small affair with just the three of us round our old dining-room table. Despite the lack of fancy clothes and expensive presents, I always enjoyed spending the twenty-fifth of December with my mum and dad. No matter what had happened throughout the year, no matter what challenges we had to contend with, I could always rely on one blissful day at the end of the year. Christmas Day was a little bit like a time capsule where I knew exactly what to expect. It was Groundhog Day, but in the best way.

My parents and I would begin the morning with our usual porridge breakfast, sprinkled with cinnamon, followed by the next few hours being spent in the kitchen, listening to the radio as we peeled potatoes and whipped cream. We'd always open our presents after we'd had our Christmas lunch, which would be followed by watching the Queen's speech. After which, we'd play a number of card games before kicking back with a box of Quality Street chocolates to enjoy alongside whatever Christmas entertainment was on the television.

It's funny how everyone has a different idea of the perfect Christmas. Families have their own rituals, traditions and orders to the day. My family Christmas was a very different kind of celebration to the one I'm having this year. And today is one of those times where I can't help but think of my parents and wonder what they'd make of the Silver family.

In the new year, I will go and visit my cousins. I have a cluster on my mother's side who live up in Liverpool and two elderly cousins on my father's side who are on the other side of London. I tend to see my Liverpudlian cousins only once a year, unless there's a wedding or a funeral. But, I try to stop by and see my older cousins on the other side of London once every six weeks or so. Although I've been so wrapped up in my newly-wed life that I realise I haven't really seen anyone since my wedding in October. I must arrange some catch-ups with friends in the new year as well.

'What's for pudding?' Ronan asks.

Yasmin raises an eyebrow at him. 'Aren't you stuffed?'

'I've always got room for something sweet.' Ronan gives his wife a seductive smile.

'It's Irish cream tiramisu,' Yasmin replies.

'My favourite!' Ronan looks delighted.

It does sound like the ideal pudding to round off this Christmas dinner. I'm not quite sure how I'm going to fit any more food in. I've already eaten far more than I should have. If the wind wasn't still howling outside, I would be keen to go for a walk post-lunch to stretch out my limbs and work off some of the calories.

Yasmin brings out the Irish cream tiramisu. It looks every bit as scrumptious as it sounds. She divides up the pudding and hands me a bowl containing a generous portion. I hesitate, inhaling the strong smell of coffee. I really shouldn't eat this. I know it will cause me a major headache, and probably contains more caffeine than the average latte, but it would be super awkward to refuse to eat any. I glance around the table – everyone else is tucking in and it's clear that Jack hasn't spotted my dilemma. So I dip my spoon in some of the cream and resolve to just take a few bites to be polite.

I taste my first mouthful and it's completely delicious – the blend of coffee, cream and liqueur is heavenly. So I eat a bit more, savouring the flavours that I usually deny myself. Usually I'm so strict about my caffeine-free diet but the alcohol has softened by resolve. I'm guessing this must be one of Dawn's pre-made specials as it tastes so good. Perhaps Dawn is right and I should let go a bit more. Perhaps I've been too over-cautious by restricting caffeine completely.

I can't seem to stop myself and, before I know it, I'm scraping the bowl clean. I sit back, totally stuffed and rapidly regretting my actions immediately. The tiramisu was mouth-watering, but I really haven't had caffeine in years so I'm likely to pay for this later. I quickly guzzle down some water, hoping to hydrate myself and reduce the severity of any headache that's coming my way.

I'm relieved the meal has gone smoothly as this is the main event of the entire holiday. I exhale and silently congratulate myself as I've managed to get through an entire meal without saying or doing anything ridiculous.

'Thank you again, Yasmin,' Patrick says. 'That was the best Christmas dinner I've ever had.'

Yasmin blushes at this high praise. 'You're very welcome.' She rises from her seat and begins to collect plates from around the table.

'I'll tidy up,' I volunteer. 'You've done so much already.'

Yasmin doesn't argue and sinks back into her seat.

'I'll help,' Zara adds.

Together we clear the table while the others drift into the lounge and it's just the two of us left in the kitchen.

We work together to load the dishwasher. Soon enough, we've got the room looking spotless again. I'm feeling satisfied with our clean-up efforts and a little thrum of happiness is buzzing through me. Maybe I can fit into this family, I just need to give it some time.

'Did you see Yasmin?' Zara blurts out to me.

I frown slightly at this and turn away to hang up my dishcloth. I'm not comfortable gossiping about Yasmin when anyone could walk in on us. I hope Zara will get the message that I don't want to be drawn into the conversation if I stay quiet. But she doesn't.

'She always has to be queen bee,' Zara protests. 'I mean, anyone would think she'd cooked for a hundred people with the way everyone was carrying on about her roast dinner.'

'It was pretty good,' I reply, my insides churning as I feel more and more uneasy.

'*It was the best*,' Zara does a surprisingly close imitation of Patrick's voice. 'All she did was shove the food in the oven.'

I can't help but snigger at this.

'Zara! Stop!' I glance over my shoulder and praying no one can hear Zara impersonating Patrick. I don't think he would find it funny at all.

'*You're so welcome*,' Zara is mimicking Yasmin now, echoing her earlier words.

I can't help myself, I belly laugh. Zara sounds so convincing. And she's right, the fawning over Yasmin was all a bit much.

'*Because I'm Mrs Perfect.*' Zara twists a dishcloth in her hands with a smirk.

The kitchen door bangs open.

I jump so violently that I end up flying forward a few paces.

But it's okay, it's just Jack. And he doesn't seem to have heard. Although I'm sure if he had, my husband would be joining in. I place a hand on the worktop to steady myself and take a few calming, deep breaths before looking up.

Jack has had more than a few, his face is flushed with alcohol. He's looking a little unsteady on his feet but it's Christmas Day and everyone's allowed to have a bit too much on today of all days.

'Coffee?' I ask him as he perches on a stool at the breakfast bar.

'Yes please, with Baileys in it.' My husband's smooth voice gives me goosebumps. Despite the stress and anxiety of the last few days, I can't believe how lucky I am to be here with my handsome husband, in this luxury holiday lodge. Jack and I have got our whole lives together and this is just the beginning. This holiday marks the end of one of the best years of my life. My business has been flying, I fulfilled my dream of going travelling and I married the man I love. Our new home is more than I could ever have hoped for and I have a brand new family. Everything is as dreamy as it could possibly be.

So why can't I shake the feeling that something's not quite right?

Chapter Twenty-Nine

Yasmin

Patrick has The Pogues on the record player and is singing tunelessly along to 'Dirty Old Town'. We've all had our fill of drinks today, including me. Although I've had to drink discreetly, taking surreptitious sips of prosecco when no one's paying too much attention. Ronan – and Patrick – still both believe that I'm pregnant. And, for now, I don't want to correct them. The way I see it, I'm giving Patrick some hope. Something to look forward to. He cherishes his granddaughter and I've no doubt he would dote on another grandchild as well. It's very possible that next month I might fall pregnant. I cross my fingers hard at this thought.

Dawn is sitting on Patrick's lap now, draping herself across him in the way that she does, which is totally inappropriate, but she doesn't seem to care. At least he's stopped his singing now. Ronan and Jack are both dancing about like loons. Zara and Alicia are drinking in the corner, they clink their glasses at something. Alicia throws back her head and laughs loudly, before sliding her eyes in my direction. I have the unsettling feeling they're talking about me. But I shake the idea away.

Baby Lily is in her cot upstairs and she's fast asleep. It's been a busy day and a long one too. I smile as I watch Ronan and Jack messing about. With the music in the background, the alcohol flowing and the family all together, it's times like this that I can almost forget our financial woes. This feels like a brief moment when everything is frozen in time and my worries are suspended in mid-air. They're still there, shimmering above me like a rain cloud, but, for now, I allow myself to separate out from them. To step off the frantic hamster wheel I seem to have been on in the last few months and to shrug off all my concerns and relax a little.

Ronan and Jack are now attempting to do an Irish jig. It's probably been years since either of them successfully performed any Irish dancing where alcohol wasn't involved. Their arms are entwined, their feet flying. Patrick and Dawn are clapping them. I join in and so do Zara and Alicia. Ronan and Jack quickly become breathless with exertion and then Jack staggers, knocking into Ronan, and they both end up falling over each other. They land in a tangle of limbs on the sofa.

We all clap madly and then Ronan stands up and takes a bow. He sees me flushed with laughter and steps towards me. His breath is hot and heavy with the smell of beer.

'Come 'ere,' he says in a low growl before landing me a kiss on the lips.

I pull away from him, a recent habit. Things have been so up and down between us lately.

Ronan shrugs off my rejection and crosses the room to grab his can of drink. I notice my husband pulling his phone out of the pocket of his chinos. He checks the screen and immediately stuffs the phone back. At least the lack of signal has stopped Ronan going on his phone since the connection has been down. I swear he's addicted to that device. I can tell he's getting antsy at the lack of contact with the outside world. We agreed between us to leave the issue of Wi-Fi and phone connection to tomorrow. It's been a few days now, but, realistically, there's no point in trying to get things sorted on Christmas Day.

At least it's given us the opportunity to properly disconnect from work. That's the problem these days, it's so easy to have a quick look at your email inbox or check the latest notification that's buzzed through. It's been a bit of a relief to not have the lure of the laptop or the interruption of a ringing phone for a bit.

Jack and Ronan are back up and dancing in the middle of the room again. I go and join them, taking my husband's hands and smiling at him. I was too quick to push him away earlier. There's been so much strain on us both in the last few months due to the problems with the business.

Patrick and Dawn join us and we all dance about for another song or two, until Jack pushes past me and makes a hasty retreat from the room. I assume by his manner that his alcohol intake has finally got the better of him and he's off to be sick in the toilet bowl.

I sit down, feeling suddenly tired, and check the baby monitor. Lily is still sleeping soundly, despite the noise we're making down here. I fiddle with the white gold locket around my neck. It was a touching gift from Ronan but I hope he didn't pay too much for it.

'Oooh, look!' Dawn points out of the floor-to-ceiling window. 'Fireworks.'

We all gather in front of the glass as the pitch-black sky lights up with greens and golds.

'So pretty!' Dawn exclaims.

'I wonder who's setting them off?' Zara asks.

'Could be down at The Mount,' Patrick answers.

The sky glows once more, this time with blue and purple colours. We all stand transfixed, holding our breath for the next round of the display. The crackle and fizzle of the fireworks fade away. I begin to think there will be no more and then, suddenly: boom! A rocket whooshes upwards and the sky's ablaze with every colour of the rainbow.

'Wow,' Alicia breathes. 'That's quite something.'

And she's right. It's magical as the fireworks display reaches its crescendo. They're absolutely stunning and a gorgeous way to end our Christmas Day. I realise that Ronan has his arm around me and we stand there, leaning against each other, until the night returns to a black, blank canvas once more.

It has been an important day for me: Lily's first Christmas and my first 25th of December as a mother. I'm proud of myself for not only rescuing the roast dinner but doing so in a way that resulted in such praise.

I'm pleased for Patrick that today has been a good one. A special Christmas for him at such a difficult time and a keepsake memory for the rest of the family. None of us really know what the future holds. This might be Patrick's last festive vacation or he might outlive us all.

The only thing that I do know is that often when things are on a high they have to come crashing back down again. And I suspect that's what's going to happen next...

Chapter Thirty

Alicia

It's only when the fireworks draw to a close that I realise my husband has not returned to the lounge. He wasn't amongst our little cluster as we oooohed and ahhhhhhed at the display flashing in the sky. So where is he? Perhaps he's decided to call it a night already and has crashed out on our bed upstairs. But surely he wouldn't have gone up without letting me know?

Dawn smiles. 'It's been lovely. Thank you, everyone. I'm going to head up to the land of Nod now.'

'Happy Christmas!' I say.

Dawn retreats from the room.

It has been a nice day. I'm starting to warm to the Silver family. Sure, they have their quirks and flaws just like any family. But the difference is they're my family now. And I've resolved to embrace them as such. I just hope that they will accept me too.

I'm just about to open my mouth to say goodnight to everyone else when a shriek from the hallway pierces through the chatter in the lounge.

'What the—' Patrick is barrelling through the door in seconds. 'Dawn, are you okay?' he shouts.

There's a muffled reply and then an almighty crash. I look at Zara and Zara looks back at me; bewilderment is written across both of our faces.

'Dad, Dad, what's going on?' Ronan squeezes into the dimly lit hallway, followed by Yasmin and me.

Initially, I can't see anything in the darkness of the hallway but gradually my eyes adjust to the lack of light. I can make out a figure on the floor. My heart jolts when I realise it's Jack. He's collapsed on the wooden flooring.

'Jack!'

Yasmin and Ronan shrink back to allow me to pass by them and someone clicks on the light.

'Are you okay? Are you unwell?'

'I nearly broke my neck falling over him!' Dawn's voice is high-pitched.

'Just get up,' Patrick barks at his son. He extends a hand towards Jack but my husband rolls in the opposite direction and vomits.

'Urgh!' Yasmin clearly has no sympathy. 'Disgusting,' I hear her mutter before she makes a dash for the stairs and hurries up to the next floor.

I'm cross with her response, her lack of concern. I'm sure she's no angel. We've all done it; had a bit too much to drink and then paid the consequences.

I kneel down and pat my husband's leg. 'I'll grab something to clean up with!' I hop up and move as quickly as I can to the kitchen.

There's a cupboard stocked up with disinfectant, a mop and a bucket so I get to work gathering everything I need.

I'm almost done when I hear raised voices. I clatter back out into the hallway with the cleaning materials in my hands.

'Look at the state o' you, boy,' Patrick is sneering at Jack. 'You're a disgrace.'

I survey the situation. I agree that Jack's drinking has got a bit out of hand but I think Patrick is being a bit harsh.

'How dare you behave like this in my house,' Patrick continues before roughly grabbing Jack's shirt in his meaty fists and dragging him up to standing. 'Can you even understand me?'

Jack's eyes look glassy and unfocused. He clearly isn't taking in everything his father is saying.

I step in. 'Patrick, don't worry, I'll get him up to bed and clean up. It's easily sorted.'

'Is it?' Patrick barks back.

My eyes are wide and uncomprehending. This can't be the first time they've witnessed Jack going a bit overboard with drink.

'Is this your influence?' Patrick turns his attention to me, his lip curled in disdain.

'My influence?' I stutter, wondering what he means.

'She might not know,' Dawn says to Patrick gently, laying a calming hand on his arm.

Patrick releases his hold on Jack, who totters backwards and sits down heavily on the first step of the staircase.

'Know what?' I ask.

Dawn gives Patrick a warning glare and then opens the bathroom door. The overhead light is on and seems too stark and bright. Dawn gestures for me to look inside the small room.

I poke my head inside and immediately realise what the problem is. There's a tell-tale line of white powder along the deep-set windowsill. I inhale sharply.

My heart sinks.

Just when I thought we'd had the perfect day. Why is Jack back up to his old tricks?

Of course I knew Jack took recreational drugs every now and again when he was hitting the party scene in London. It was never something I got involved in myself but it was something that happened around me. So many of my acquaintances and friends experimented in their twenties, it wasn't uncommon. But I noticed that Jack dabbled more than most. I worried for him but it was his choice. I wasn't his keeper, so I turned a blind eye. That was until about two years ago when I noticed that Jack was relying a little too heavily on manufactured highs. I tried to help him, to talk to him and to encourage him to seek professional advice but he refused to see that he had a problem. Things began to change between us and it was Jack's increasingly erratic behaviour which sent me off on my journey of soul searching in Thailand. With us both being in London, it was all too easy for me to continue in the same pattern with him. Trying to get him to see that he needed to stop but still unable to resist being in his company whenever I could. Travelling was a chance for me to put some distance between us, so I could figure out what I really wanted and break my own addiction to Jack. When I came back and Jack proposed, he promised me the mistakes of his younger days were behind him. He wanted a fresh start, a clean slate and he told me he had sorted himself out. I believed him.

Things have been on an even keel – or so I thought. But perhaps Jack has just been deceiving me all along.

Patrick storms off and Dawn gives me a sympathetic look before following in his wake. Only Ronan stays to help me manoeuvre my spaced-out husband upstairs. Ronan, to his credit, then accompanies me back downstairs to help me clean up.

'Trust Jack,' Ronan says grimly.

I remain silent, a million thoughts whirring through my brain.

'Come and knock on our door if you need anything tonight. He should just sleep it off now.'

I nod and say a quiet thanks.

'The thing about my brother,' Ronan sighs, 'is that he always takes things too far...'

'I thought he'd given up...' my voice trails off. As my thoughts unscramble, it know the words I'm saying aren't necessarily true. I chose to ignore any warning signs because I wanted to believe Jack had turned a new leaf.

My husband has lied to me. And if he can lie to me about this, what else has he lied to me about?

Chapter Thirty-One

Jack

My head is pounding, the beat of a drum knocking relentlessly inside of my skull. I roll over onto my back. My mouth feels like sawdust and I'm desperate for a drink of water. I try to open my eyes but I have to try a few times before I succeed in this small effort. I'm groggy, my limbs feel like dead weights and my brain is hazy on where I am and what day it is.

I eventually manage to sit up and take in my surroundings. The duvet is twisted around my legs and I look over to the body lying next to me.

It's Alicia, she's uncovered, her figure is devoid of any blankets, and she's shivering slightly in her thin nightdress.

'Sorry,' I say, my voice sounding deep and scratchy. 'Here.' I chuck her half of the duvet back to her. As I focus my eyes, I realise that Alicia isn't half asleep, her eyes are wide open and she has a troubled expression on her face. She's positioned in a rigid and unnatural way, her hair fans out on the pillow beneath her and her limbs are tense.

Something isn't right. I reach for the glass of water on my bedside table and drain the contents before swinging my legs out of the bed. I sit for a minute, the world spinning around me, and then I curse loudly. I know why my wife is lying wide awake in our bed and looking so stressed out. The events of last night flood through my mind and I groan.

It had been such a perfect Christmas Day, everything had gone so well. And then I ruined it. I have a vision of myself in a heap outside the downstairs bathroom. I remember the faces of my family staring down at me. Their concern rapidly turned to anger when my father discovered the white line of powder on the windowsill.

I swear. And then I swear again.

Alicia says nothing. I turn to look at her once more. She's staring resolutely at the ceiling now. Her not saying anything makes me feel even worse.

'Last night...' I begin before trailing off. There's nothing I can say to defend myself. I hit the bottle too hard yesterday and then decided to take things too far. I should've known better than to try to get away with something like that right under my father's nose.

I groan once more. I'm going to have to grovel a lot. I was meant to be getting into my father's good books, not giving him a reason to add another black mark against my name. I have no idea how I'm going to turn this around. Firstly, I need to apologise to Alicia.

'I'm sorry,' I whisper half-heartedly to Alicia. 'I was stupid.'

She looks at me and rolls her eyes.

'You're not sorry,' she replies in a monotone voice. 'You're just sorry you got caught.'

There's no use denying it, she's right.

'What am I going to do now?'

Alicia closes her eyes, as if to shut out the problem.

'I'm going to need your help,' I say.

Alicia rolls over, propping herself up on her elbow. 'What kind of help?'

'Help apologising to my father.'

'How about dealing with the problem?

'What do you mean?'

'Well, I think this is something that is going to take more than an apology to fix. Your father will want you to do something about it. You're going to have to stop messing around with all that stuff now. You need to break the habit.'

Her words sink in. I hadn't even thought about that. My main concern was how to go about making things up to my father. Alicia is right again, actions will mean more than words. It's not something I want to have to deal with. I can at least start by saying I'll put an end to my recreational habits. It's not like I'm an addict – well, I don't think I am. I'm sure I could stop any time if I really wanted to. I just don't want to. But I'm going to have to try now, in order to patch things up with my father. It's the only way.

I shower and dress slowly. Alicia and I then make our way downstairs and I'm dreading the thought of facing everyone. The disapproving looks and the judgement are not something I want to face on a hangover like this one.

We go into the kitchen and as soon as I step through the door, I open my mouth and begin my apology. 'Dad, I'm sorry...'

He's pacing up and down by the bifold windows. He puts one hand up to stop the flow of my words. His face is lined with worry. I pause, sensing this is going to go very badly. Taking in my father standing there, silencing me with a hand gesture makes my blood boil. The truth is, I hate his guts. I can't stand the man. Not after the way he treated my poor mother. He treated her appallingly and, when it got too much, he cast her aside and divorced her. She had her faults, but she didn't deserve to be kicked out of the family home because my father couldn't be bothered to support her when she needed it the most. She was an alcoholic but it wasn't her fault. It was his. If she'd been married to someone who treated her better, I'm sure things would've been different.

I tried to help my mother but I was still young. I didn't have the means to ensure she was well-looked after. But he did. That's why I keep the man that is my father at arm's length. Ronan seemed to be able to forget the way he treated our mother but I can't.

I bite my lip and try to keep the anger that's simmering inside me contained.

'We were just about to come and get you guys,' Ronan says. He also looks uncharacteristically anxious.

I wait for him to continue.

'Something's happened.'

'What's the matter?' Alicia steps forward.

Ronan frowns. 'Dawn's gone.'

'What do you mean she's gone?' I ask.

'She's not here, no one has seen her at all this morning. She went up to bed last night. Dad said he fell asleep when she was in the en-suite. But she's not here now.'

'Have you seen her?' Yasmin asks, looking at me and Alicia.

'No,' I reply swiftly. 'We've only just got up.'

Yasmin nods, as if expecting this response.

'Did you see her during the night at all?' Patrick queries.

'No, we both went straight to sleep and we've only just woken up. Isn't that right, Alicia?'

My wife agrees and the room falls silent.

'Perhaps she's gone for a walk,' I suggest.

'She wouldn't go by herself, not in these conditions,' Patrick says.

'Well, has anyone been outside and actually checked?' I query.

Ronan shakes his head.

'You're right, we should all go and look for her. She might have gone to take a photo or something and slipped and fallen.' My father hastily downs the rest of his coffee and dumps the cup in the sink.

'I don't suppose your phone signal is working?' Yasmin asks.

'No,' Alicia and I both echo together.

Yasmin sighs. 'If only the phones were working, I'm sure we'd be able to get hold of her quickly.'

The clock is showing half past eight. I can't imagine Dawn would have got up early to go for a walk. Unless she couldn't sleep? My father is an early riser and Dawn isn't usually up before him.

'Right, Yasmin, you stay here,' my father commands. 'Just in case Dawn comes back while we're out looking for her.'

'I'll come with you to look for her,' I offer.

He hesitates and I can tell he doesn't really want to be paired with me.

'I'll go with Ronan,' Alicia follows up. She's obviously understood that I want to have some time to speak with my father.

'Good plan,' Ronan says.

Zara is sitting in the corner of the room, looking out of the window. She swivels round, 'What should I do?'

'Stay here with Yasmin,' Patrick tells her. 'Keep trying on the phone.'

Zara isn't an outdoors sort of person and she doesn't know these mountains so I can see why Patrick has told her to stay put. Zara stares back out the window, lost in thought. Dawn is the only family she has so this must be hard for her.

There's a flurry of activity as the four of us haul on our outdoor layers. I grab a slice of toast from the plate Yasmin holds out to me and gulp down a cup of sweet tea.

'Here's some flasks,' Yasmin says, handing out the containers of tea that she's just made up. 'Hopefully you won't be too long. It's so cold out there.'

I'm not relishing the thought of trudging outside in the snowy weather but Dawn's disappearance has shifted my family's focus away from my misdemeanours last night.

I step outside the front door and the temperature hits me. The wind is bitingly cold and I appreciate my thick winter layers. I survey the misty morning skyline ahead of me. All appears calm and undisturbed. The cars are still parked in the same place they've been for the last few days, tucked away in a garage to the side of the lodge. I notice there aren't any footprints anywhere in my eyeline. Our nearest neighbours are miles away and if Dawn had been outside recently, she would surely have left a trail of footprints. As there aren't any, I can only assume that she left the lodge long enough ago for the footprints to be covered in fresh snow. But why did she leave? And where is she now?

'Are you sure she's not inside somewhere?' Alicia asks doubtfully.

'I've searched everywhere,' my father growls back.

'We'll go down the hill,' Ronan tells me. 'You and Dad take the woodland area.'

'Fine.'

I lean forward and try to give Alicia a peck on the cheek but she turns away from me. I was foolish to think she'd forgive me that quickly.

I watch as my wife and my brother stride away from me. Alicia is already calling Dawn's name.

'We'll find her,' I say to my father, trying to reassure him.

He grunts. 'We'd better do.'

I think his response is a little odd. The whole thing feels off – why would Dawn leave the lodge without telling anyone? And how will we find her in this weather?

Chapter Thirty-Two

Alicia

I'm counting down the days until this holiday is over. It couldn't have been any more disastrous. I've made so many errors, Jack has disgraced himself with his behaviour and now Dawn has gone missing. This was not what I was expecting from my first family holiday with Jack's family. When he showed me pictures of the place, I was so excited. It looks completely idyllic, the perfect place to spend Christmas. But it's been anything but perfect.

Now I'm in the freezing cold, shouting into the ether, with no real idea of where Dawn might be. It doesn't make any sense. Why would she go outside in this awful weather by herself? It's not snowing at the moment but we had another heavy load last night. Everywhere we look is just a pure blanket of white. There's no sign of anyone or anything as far as I can see. The hill curves downwards and there's a thick mist hanging in the air all around us.

Ronan and I get further and further away from the lodge. He's walking quickly and I'm finding it difficult to keep up with his long strides.

'Can we stop for a second?'

Ronan comes to a halt immediately. 'Is everything okay?'

'Yeah, I just need to catch my breath.'

'Oh, sorry. Am I going too fast?'

'Just a bit.' I grimace, holding my side. I ate so much yesterday and I haven't been my usual active self in the last few days. So it's no wonder my body is protesting at this sudden burst of energy.

I look back over my shoulder. Bartley Lodge already looks small in the distance behind us. A warm light glows in the front window and I wish I was back inside right now.

Ronan shuffles his feet impatiently.

'Do you think she would have gone this way?' I question.

'I don't know why she'd leave the house at all to be honest.'

So Ronan is wondering the same thing as me.

'Where does this road lead to?'

'This is the main route down from this section of the mountain. It curves back towards the nearest village. It's the way we went to The Mount.'

'Ah.' I have absolutely no sense of direction at the best of times. This is new territory for me and, with the snow everywhere, there's no distinctive landmarks around to help me figure out where we are.

'Ready?' Ronan presses.

My brother-in-law is obviously eager to set off again. I can understand his logic in following the main road but I still can't work out why Dawn would head this way. It's not like she would pop out for milk. We have everything we need at the lodge and the nearest village is miles away, so I can't see why she would walk such a stretch by herself.

We set off once more. I rack my brains to try to come up with a topic of conversation. I don't know Ronan very well and I haven't identified much common ground between us yet. Although, he's marching ahead so fast that it's all I can do to keep up with him. I soon find that I don't have the breath to talk anyway.

I start to fall behind but I don't want to voice my need to pause again. Ronan is on a mission and I feel like I'm holding him back.

After a few more minutes, Ronan notices the widening gap between us. He stops and I pump my legs harder to catch up with him. I'm red-faced and breathless by the time I reach him.

Ronan sweeps his eyes over me. 'I'll go ahead and see if I can locate her,' he tells me. 'You keep walking in this direction. We will head back the same way we've come, just follow the road.'

'Okay,' I say, although I don't feel very comfortable about us splitting up. I don't want to slow him down though, especially if Dawn is in any kind of trouble. She may have fallen and sprained her ankle or something. I'm sure once she's found this will be something that we'll all laugh about in years to come but right now she might need help, so I let Ronan speed off without any further conversation.

I walk at a steadier pace now that I'm not trying to keep up with Ronan. I know I'm also going to have to walk back up this hill to get back to the lodge, so I need to make sure I don't use up my energy.

I take the thermal flask from the rucksack on my back and drink some of the lukewarm tea inside. It tastes way too milky, but I drink it anyway, grateful for the small amount of warmth. I have a stabbing pain above my left eye, it's been increasing in intensity in the last hour and I'm sure it's the result of the caffeine-loaded tiramisu yesterday. What I really need is a couple of big glasses of water but the tea is all I have with me. Yet more caffeine, which is likely to make my headache worse, but I've got no choice. And it's so cold, I'll take any warmth I can get.

Ronan has disappeared around a bend in the road. I hope he finds Dawn so that we can all get back to the lodge sooner rather than later. At this point, I'm past caring why Dawn left and just feeling eager for her to be found so I can spend the rest of the afternoon in front of the TV and the blazing fireplace.

'Where are you Dawn?' I mutter to myself.

I scan the horizon once more. The morning mist is starting to lift a little but visibility is still poor. The snow stretches out on either side of the dirt track that acts as the main route down from the lodge. I can't see anything from where I'm standing. And I definitely can't see Dawn.

I keep walking on and on. I check my phone and the time shows me I've been outdoors for an hour. This is ridiculous. I peer in front of me but there's no sign of Ronan, he's long gone. I stand for a minute, contemplating what to do. Should I keep going or turn back?

I decide to turn back. I've done my share of looking and Ronan said we would be walking the same route back. He moves much faster than I do, so I want to give myself a head start on the slow and painful journey back up the steep hill.

Another half an hour goes by and my energy is really flagging. The cold feels like it's seeping into my bones. I realise I should've turned around much sooner. There's no sign of Ronan still and I'm making even slower progress going back up the hill than I was coming down it.

I hear a twig snap and I jump. I look around me wildly but there's no one else there. Only me.

I'm getting a bit jittery now. The mist swirling around me feels oppressive and ominous. My limbs are screaming for a rest but I don't want to be out here by myself for a second longer than I need to be.

Another twig snaps.

I have this horrible feeling that someone is watching me. I whirl round and take in my surroundings once more. Everything is still serene and undisturbed. It feels eerie to be out here like this without company. It's like I'm the only person left on this patch of earth, and I really don't like it. I'm used to being in the city, amongst the hustle and bustle of crowds. It's very rare that I'm ever alone like this.

The hairs on my neck are standing on end, I'm feeling spooked. The uncertainty pooling in the pit of my stomach spurs me on. The slope in front of me seems steeper with every step.

I try to shake away my worry. There's no one nearby. Just me and the endless stretch of snow.

I don't know where Dawn is or what's happened to her but I've done my bit. I just want to get back to Bartley Lodge, pack my bags and head home to London as soon as I possibly can, before this Christmas holiday gets any worse.

Chapter Thirty-Three

Yasmin

I watch out of the window as Jack and Patrick march towards the woodland area in front of the lodge. They're walking in tandem, matching each other, with their arms swinging by their sides and their long legs covering the unblemished ground in front of them. Ronan and Alicia are heading towards the dirt-track road that curves down the mountain towards the nearest village. My husband is striding ahead and Alicia is trotting behind him, trying to keep up.

I'm glad that I'm not out there. Lily is the perfect excuse for me to stay at Bartley Lodge. She's in the middle of the lounge now, rolling a toy ball back and forth across the floor. She has so many new presents to play with but this is the one that has captured her attention this morning. I go and sit down on the floor opposite my little girl. I grab the soft ball and push it back to her. She squeals, excited to have my attention. I lose myself in child's play, watching Lily's face light up every time her chubby hands grasp the smooth material of the toy. This interaction allows me to take my mind off the current situation for a few minutes. I'm worried about Dawn. Despite the recent cooling of our relationship, I'm concerned. This is so unlike her.

I snap a photo of Lily and check my phone signal for the twentieth time that morning. Still nothing.

We continue playing together. The minutes tick by and then the lounge door creaks open.

I spin around, hoping to see Dawn coming through the door. Perhaps there's a perfectly reasonable explanation for her disappearance. Or maybe we didn't search the house thoroughly enough and she's been here all along.

But it's not Dawn, it's Zara.

'Oh, hi Zara.'

'Are they back yet?' she enquires.

'They've not been gone that long.'

'Fifteen minutes,' she says in reply, as though she's been counting. 'I thought they were going to find her quickly. Dawn doesn't do long walks by herself, so why aren't they back?'

Zara stands at the window, her arms folded in front of her chest. I pull myself up from the floor and stand next to her. But there's no movement whatsoever. Everything is still and white.

'Don't worry,' I reply. 'They'll find her.'

'But why has she gone? Dawn wouldn't just wander off.'

I shrug my shoulders. 'Maybe she needed some air or got tired of being cooped up.'

Zara frowns back at me. She opens her mouth as if to say something and shuts it again. It's obvious that she's also feeling worried about Dawn's disappearance.

'Come on, why don't we get some lunch together so it's ready for when they return.'

Zara stares back at me. 'It's okay, I'm going to go upstairs.' She slouches out of the room.

I sigh. It really wouldn't have hurt her to put together some lunch. She's barely done anything since she got here. At most, she's made a few rounds of coffees. I scoop up Lily just as she's making a beeline for the brightly coloured Christmas baubles once more.

'I've got you.' I laugh, tickling her tummy. 'Let's go and get your lunch sorted, baby.'

In the kitchen, I strap Lily into her highchair and give her a few board books to play with. Then I start putting together a healthy salad. We've all had far too much alcohol and junk food in the last few days. So I'm looking forward to nice, refreshing green leaves and colourful vegetables. I wash the leaves and chop some tomatoes, losing myself in my thoughts as I prepare the lunch.

I have no idea where Dawn is or what she's up to. It's not like her to head off or go for an outside jaunt. If anything, she's probably organised some kind of Christmas surprise for Patrick. Maybe she went out for a delivery or something and it's taking longer than expected. I'm sure that must be the answer.

The lunch is ready but there isn't any sign of the search party yet. So I feed Lily her baby food, then give her some milk and get her down for her afternoon nap. All of this takes a bit of time and I'm absorbed in my tasks. When I'm finally through the daily ritual of feeding my daughter and putting her to bed, I'm surprised that Ronan, Alicia, Jack and Patrick still haven't returned.

I stand at the lounge window and gaze out at the scenery. There are footprint trails in the snow showing the path Ronan and Alicia took and the way Jack and Patrick went. The sky is grey and the clouds are still thick with snow. A few snowflakes are beginning to flutter and I'm guessing the weather is about to get worse again.

Perhaps I shouldn't have sent Ronan off so easily. He only had a hot flask and a few snacks in his rucksack. I really didn't think they'd be this long. I was sure Dawn couldn't have got far.

I flick through TV channels but nothing catches my interest. I can't concentrate properly and so I just keep scrolling through, half-watching ads and trailers but not really engaging with what's on screen. I have one ear trained on the door but there's no sign of anyone. Zara is still shut up in her room I decide not to call her down. I can't face making small talk with her at the best of times, let alone in such a tense situation.

Several times I go and stand at the window again, looking out and wondering where everyone has got to. The sun is high in the sky now, it's well past midday and I'm getting more worried. It's frustrating that the phone line and the internet are still down. We're completely cut off here and there's no way of contacting each other. I feel more stressed because of this.

And then I hear the front door being pushed open. I fly towards it and see Patrick and Jack's faces. Both of them are sporting red noses and watery eyes.

'Gosh, you must be freezing. I wondered where you'd got to!'

I peer around the two figures but it's just them.

'Are Ronan and Alicia not with you?'

'Have they not come back?' Jack says, frowning.

'No...'

Jack looks puzzled. 'But we've been gone for hours.'

'I know, what took you so long?'

'We haven't found Dawn,' Patrick says flatly. 'It was my fault we were out so long, I wanted to make sure we'd checked all through the trees thoroughly. There was no sign of her.'

'No sign whatsoever,' Jack confirms.

I sigh, this wasn't the news I was hoping for.

'Come in, lunch is ready.'

The two men get themselves seated at the wooden kitchen table and wolf down their food. I realise now that I should have made something more filling for them.

'So you haven't heard anything from Ronan or Alicia then?' Jack asks, through a mouthful of salad leaves.

I shake my head.

Time seems to drag on. We search the house once more but Dawn is nowhere to be seen. And there's no clues either. I flick through Dawn's wardrobe, trying to see if I can work out what clothes she might be wearing but she has so many different outfits, it's impossible to guess. We have coffee and we each keep watch at the window. Ronan and Alicia are both still out there in the freezing temperature. I'm starting to realise it was stupid of us to send more people out into the snowy weather when it was obvious that Dawn hadn't merely gone for a stroll nearby. But with no phone signal and no other houses for miles around, it was the only option we had.

The sun is lower in the sky now. It won't be long until the winter sun starts to set. It's crazy that Ronan and Alicia have been gone for so long. Something must have happened to them. I feel dizzy at the thought of my husband out there in this weather. I cross my fingers and will him to walk through the door. But I'm not likely to manifest him back to me so I need to take action.

I pull my phone out of my pocket and, finally, I can see two little bars of signal. I daren't move from the spot I'm in, in case I lose it again. So I just yell Jack and Patrick's names. They both come speeding into the lounge.

'What is it?' Jack asks breathlessly.

'I've got some signal.'

'Great, try Dawn's number,' Patrick urges.

I do as he asks. The dialling tone kicks in but it just rings and rings. There's no answer.

'I'll call Ronan.' I press the phone to my ear but his phone just goes straight to voicemail.

'Try Alicia now,' Jack suggests.

There's no answer from my sister-in-law either. I repeat this several times, ringing the same three numbers over and over but there's no response.

I can see the snow beginning to fall at a faster rate outside, as the light begins to fade. So there's only one number left to call.

'Police please.'

Chapter Thirty-Four

Alicia

I trudge through the snow, my breath coming out in puffs, visible in front of me in the frosty air. I scan the hazy horizon; I can barely see anything past the end of my own outstretched hand.

My feet sink into the clean snow. There are no other footprints, no one else has been here for some time. So where is everybody? How have I managed to get so lost?

I was sure that I'd stuck to the dirt road, like Ronan told me to. But, in some places, it was hard to see underneath the ice and snow if I was still on track. I must have veered off course without realising it.

I keep walking, slow, heavy steps. My boots are weighing me down and my body aches with the effort it takes to keep going. I can't stop, I need to get back to the lodge, otherwise I'll freeze to death out here.

The snow is coming down hard now and, just as I start to despair, I see a light in the distance. It must be the holiday lodge. It has to be.

I stumble forward, eager to get inside, to find warmth. Then I see something in the snow, just ahead of me – a flash of colour. As I get nearer, I can see a still and unmoving shape on the ground. It's unmistakeable.

A body.

Spread out like a snow angel, hair fanning out across the white, soft blanket beneath it. A trickle of bright red blood from mouth to cheek, frozen in a moment of time. It looks unnatural, someone has positioned the person in exactly this way to make a statement.

My mouth hangs open in shock. I blink rapidly. Surely I must be seeing things? Hallucinating because I'm tired and cold and hungry. I'm not near enough to recognise who it is but I don't want to go any closer.

That's when I hear the sirens. Two police cars are moving a little way off to my right; they must be going along the road that I was meant to be following. The blue flashing lights get brighter. They look as though they're heading towards the lodge. But then they stop. They've seen me.

My first thought is one of relief – people are on their way. I'm was beginning to think I wouldn't get back to safety.

My second thought is much darker. More fearful. My gaze snags back to the shape in the snow. It's definitely there. I'm not imagining it.

And then the German shepherd Garda dogs rush towards me, followed by the shouts of men in uniform.

They speed closer, the gap between us narrowing by the second. I'm clearly the target but, any minute now, they're also going to spot the lifeless figure on the ground in front of me.

They will find me.

And they will find the dead body too.

I panic. How is this happening? I'm on my own, I've been wandering around in this cold wilderness for hours and I don't have anyone to account for my movements.

This doesn't look good. At all.

One of the canines skids to a halt in front of me. His companion keeps running and stops by the body that's becoming more and more covered by the fresh layer of snow. The dog barks sharply three times and then sits, as if guarding the prone figure.

What do I do now? Just stand here, waiting for the Garda to reach me and face the consequences?

Every fibre in my body is screaming at me to run. To get away from this situation as fast as I can. This doesn't feel right; I'm not meant to be here. This is the wrong time, wrong place for me in the worst way possible.

I can't move. I know it won't take much for the dogs and the officers to catch up with me. I'm exhausted as it is and I don't have a lot of energy left. I'll also make myself look even more guilty if I flee. So I stand, rigid as an ice statue, waiting for the inevitable. Waiting for the sting of the words from the arresting officers.

I didn't do this.

This had nothing to do with me.

I'm not a killer.

But will they believe me?

The lights, the barking animals and the new voices of the uniformed offices coming towards me, all overlapping one another, are overwhelming. I've spent most of the day in total silence, in a world of white, and now I'm getting sensory overload.

I put my hands up to shield my face and I back away slightly from the big dog that's metres from me. Its lips are curled back and it's growling. My fear notches up a level.

Then everything happens at once, in a total blur. Two police officers are upon me; they see the body, they shout. There's a huge commotion as they realise there's more to the scene than they first thought.

The handcuffs bite into my wrists as I'm half lifted, half dragged between two burly Garda officers. My teeth are chattering from the cold and the fear welling up inside me.

I'm vaguely aware of one of the officers reading me my rights, it feels so surreal. Words from TV programmes and films floating in the chill air. 'You do not have to say anything...'

I couldn't say anything even if I tried. The shock at finding the dead body and then being immediately arrested, accused of murder, has resulted in my brain freezing, unable to respond to what's going on around me.

I let my body go limp and allow myself to be spirited across the snow with no resistance. Bartley Lodge is now in sight, warm light emitting from the windows and reminding me that, just a few hours ago, everything was normal. Now nothing will ever be the same again.

One of the officers shoulders open the front door and shoves me inside.

I stumble and trip, flat on my face, my arms bound behind me and unable to break my fall. A pain sears in my cheekbone and tears spring up in my eyes. I want to cry out, but I've lost all control of my voice. An officer hauls me back to my feet.

I blink rapidly to clear my eyes and when my vision unmists, I see four shocked faces staring at me from the other end of the hallway.

'What's going on?' a voice demands.

If only I could explain...

Chapter Thirty-Five

Jack

The door has just burst open and the Garda are spilling through it. I'm glad they're finally here. Amidst the commotion of a group of new people filling the entranceway, it takes me a moment to see they have someone with them.

Someone I know very well.

My wife.

She is shaking like a leaf. But the Garda officers are doing nothing to help. Alicia is pale-faced because her hands are firmly behind her back, clasped by handcuffs.

'What's going on?' I demand.

I stride across the room, closing the distance between myself and the cluster of people at the entrance to the lodge.

'What's going on?' I repeat. 'The handcuffs?' I gesture towards them. 'Are they really necessary?'

The oldest officer steps forward. He has a grey beard and grey eyes. 'I'm afraid they are. Is there a room we can use?'

'For what?'

The officer replies with authority. 'All of you will need to be split up. We need to speak with you individually to establish who's missing. It will be hours until we can get you all down to the station because of the weather.'

'What has happened?' I feel like I'm in the dark here, there's a piece of the puzzle I'm not getting. 'Where are the other two?' I snap. 'Where are Ronan and Dawn? Surely we should make sure everyone gets back here first?'

The officer gives me a long, cold, hard stare. 'We have more officers still searching. We need to move quickly to find the missing person.'

Thank God. It was ridiculous of us to organise a search party. We were trying to find Dawn. None of us thought it would be so difficult. And the situation is even worse now that more than one of our party is unaccounted for. Although the officer said 'person' and not 'people'. I wonder if it was an error or if something else is going on.

I watch as the Garda officer takes charge, organising my family to be split up, to go into different rooms, isolated from one another.

My brain is fuzzy with too little sleep. It's only then it strikes me: if Alicia is in handcuffs, then a crime must have been committed.

But what has happened?

An officer directs me towards the lounge. I sit down on the sofa, in the same place that Alicia and I were cuddled up on only the day before.

'Why is my wife is in handcuffs?'

'I can't answer that.'

I huff at this. Why can't she just tell me?

'Can you tell me who out of your party is still not accounted for?'

The police officer draws a small notepad and pen out of her top pocket.

'Yes... Ronan, my brother. He went out this morning to look for our stepmother.'

'And your stepmother is?'

'Dawn Silver.'

'And Dawn hasn't returned either?'

'No. When we woke up this morning, she wasn't here. We don't know why. A few of us went out to look for her, but she hasn't been found yet.'

'Okay,' the officer says slowly. 'I'm going to need to rewind a little. Can you tell me the names of everyone staying here?'

I want to protest at this. Sitting here with me going over everything isn't going to help find Ronan or Dawn. I manage to bite my tongue and hold back my retort. Instead, I nod and comply.

I answer in a measured fashion. I'm careful with the wording of my responses.

The policewoman continues asking me questions to establish who is on the holiday, how we're all related and to double-check that everyone apart from Dawn and Ronan are accounted for.

My answers are all brief. The Garda officer gives me a long stare and then scribbles something down in her notepad. I just hope she doesn't ask me any tricky questions about how the holiday has been going or if there had been any arguments. What do I say if she does? That there's been an undercurrent of tension the whole time we've been here?

Should I be honest and divulge all of our family rivalries and the messy relationships that we have? Do I confess that I was the cause of a massive argument last night?

My brain is on overdrive. And then I remember that, technically, I can't be questioned too much at this point. A friend of a friend is a barrister and I know that I need to be at a police station to be properly interviewed about any crime that has taken place. So this officer won't be able to ask me more than the basics. I exhale with temporary relief.

Until I know what's going on and why Alicia is in handcuffs, I'm not going to say anything more than I have to. I'm going to keep my lips sealed until I have a lawyer present. I'm pretty sure that my father won't say anything unnecessary to get me or Alicia into trouble. I may not be his favourite person in the world but it's not his style to go broadcasting family issues to anyone, let alone telling the police about our family matters. I'm not sure I can say the same about Yasmin and Zara though. At any point, either of them could mention the argument that I was at the heart of last night. I just hope Ronan and Dawn are found quickly and nothing terrible has happened. Hopefully this is all just one big misunderstanding.

The officer looks at me with her beady eyes, I can tell that she wants to probe more but she stops once she's established the whereabouts of everyone. We lapse into an excruciatingly uncomfortable silence. I wonder how long I'm going to be sat in this room for. My thoughts turn to my wife. Alicia is honest, kind and generous. I've never seen her be anything but a decent human being. But the police clearly think that she's done something awful. They must do to have her in handcuffs.

I know I should be protesting more about my wife's treatment. The Garda officer is probably intrigued as to why I'm not asking to see Alicia or pressing the issue of her arrest more. I'm her husband and I should be Alicia's greatest champion. But I have to be careful with what I say here. I don't want the police digging too much into my own complicated affairs. So I make a decision: I'm going to do all I can to save my own skin. If Alicia has done something, I'm not going to put my neck on the line for her. Alicia didn't marry a selfless man. She married me.

The officer finally stands up. 'Would you like some water?'

'Yeah, thanks,' I answer distractedly, trying to process the events of today.

She leaves the room and I hear the female Garda officer as she pauses outside the door. She's talking to one of her colleagues in hushed tones. But she's not keeping her voice down as much as she thinks she is, because I hear her say: 'We have to be careful, she might turn violent and backup won't be here for a while in this weather.'

Who are they talking about?

I listen intently, and I don't catch the response. But I do hear the first officer say something that chills me to the core.

'Someone has been murdered. Any one of them could be the killer. But my money's on her.'

Chapter Thirty-Six

Alicia

It wasn't me.

Will anyone listen to me?

Jack is standing just metres apart from me in the hallway and yet he feels a million miles away. He looks shocked, stunned. And he won't meet my gaze. Does he really think I'm guilty? Capable of murder? If my own husband doesn't believe that I'm not a killer then what hope have I got of convincing everyone else that I'm innocent?

The events of today are a blur. Why did I agree to go out in the snow, searching for Dawn? I shouldn't have got involved. I should have stayed indoors. But I was too eager to help with the search party. Too eager to try to become one of the family.

And why did I agree to go with Ronan? I hardly know the man. Why didn't Jack insist that we stick together?

Now Dawn is dead. And Ronan is missing. Out there, somewhere in the freezing wilderness beyond the lodge. Surely he's okay? Surely he will come back alive?

But what if he doesn't? Will the finger be pointed at me again if something has happened to my brother-in-law? After all, they know I was the last person to be seen with him.

I curse myself for getting wrapped up in a world I don't understand. Now I'm paying the price for love.

I'm taken to the office at the front of the lodge. When I first stepped in here I was in awe of how sumptuous everything was. Now I never want to step foot in this place ever again. I just want to go home. But will I be allowed to?

Nausea swirls in my stomach. Two police officers are in the room with me and, even though this is a decent-sized space, it feels claustrophobic with the two brawny officers. The handcuffs are still firmly in place and I wonder if this treatment is necessary. I feel as though they already believe I'm responsible. What happened to innocent until proven guilty?

I look out of the window, trying to clear my head and order my thoughts. But the snow-topped mountain in the distance just makes me feel even more closed in.

'Do you understand that we're arresting you on suspicion of the murder of Dawn Silver?'

Hearing these words spoken again makes me shiver violently. Outside, when that sentence was first spoken, it seemed so unreal. Like a nightmare that wasn't really happening. In the solid surrounds of the lodge the words sink in more fully.

'No!' Panic courses through me, I look from one of the Garda officers to the other. 'No! It wasn't me. I didn't do anything...'

Their blank faces tell me everything I need to know. In their eyes, I'm guilty. They found me by the body in a wilderness of snow with no one else in sight and that makes me the prime suspect. I shiver as the image of Dawn laid out on the white ground forces itself into my mind. Her body positioned at an awkward angle, purple bruising around her neck and a trickle of dried red blood running from her mouth into the snow.

'We're just waiting for another car, and then you'll be taken to the station for further questioning.' The older officer, with the grey eyes and beard seems to be in charge. The younger male officer remains silent.

'I was out looking for Dawn, that's all. I didn't do anything wrong!'

My pleas are falling on unsympathetic ears. I slump down on the office chair. Having my hands fastened behind my back is knocking my balance off kilter. My wrists are sore and painful, my heart is beating erratically in my chest, and the world around me feels amplified. Every sound is ringing in my ears and the bright light above is making my eyes water. They must think I'm dangerous to keep these handcuffs on.

I'm innocent. I know that but how can I get everyone else to see the truth as well?

I turn things over in my mind. I need to work out who the real killer is. That's the only way I'm going to be able to clear my name. But how? I have no idea who would do this to Dawn. Could it really be one of Jack's family? Or maybe it was a stranger? A random act of murder? If Dawn was outside by herself, especially if it was night-time, then perhaps she had a fatal encounter with an unknown person?

Yet, somehow, that line of thinking doesn't seem plausible. We're in such an isolated spot up here, even more so with all of the snow. It would make it unlikely that Dawn did fall prey to a random killer. We're not in a city, where things like that unfortunately happen all the time. We're in the Wicklow Mountains, far from the nearest village.

Somehow, I know that one member of the Silver family is responsible for Dawn's death. Someone who's been staying under this roof has blood on their hands. But who? And why would they want to kill Dawn in such a brutal way?

For the hundredth time I wish that I didn't step foot outside of the lodge this morning. And I wish that I'd never come on this Christmas holiday.

I examine each person in my mind: Patrick, Ronan, Zara, Yasmin and even Jack. If you'd asked me yesterday if any of them was a killer, I wouldn't have believed it was possible. But one of them must be.

I have nothing to go on or any evidence. All I can do is think back over the past few days. Have there been any warning signs?

My mind is blank. I despair at my impossible task.

'Please can I speak to my husband?' I beg, praying that Jack holds the answer and that he will get me out of this mess.

Because the alternative doesn't bear thinking about...

Chapter Thirty-Seven

Jack

Marry in haste, repent at leisure. That's how the saying goes. And, in this case, it's proven to be true. I thought Alicia was a safe bet, an easy solution to my problems and a marital partner that wouldn't bring too much trouble and strife with her. Instead my new wife has ruined everything.

I'm alone in the lounge now, watching the flames in the fireplace and waiting to find out what happens next. The Garda officer still hasn't returned. So I'm sitting here trying to make sense of the last few hours. I run my hands through my hair.

My reason for marrying was to appease my father and secure my inheritance. But, in a nightmarish twist, Alicia has been accused of murdering my father's wife. When I overheard the Garda officer saying that Dawn had been killed, I felt numb. It didn't take a genius to work out this is the reason why my wife is in handcuffs. Could she really be responsible for killing someone? I'm sure this must be a mistake. I'm stunned.

The woman who has been my stepmother, and part of our family for the last six years, is now dead. It's true that she wasn't my favourite person in the world, but then the woman who replaced my own mother at my father's side was never going to be my best friend.

Despite that, I wouldn't have wished her any harm. I can't believe that she's gone. Dawn was always so bubbly and so present. She lived in the moment and she tried her best to make everyone around her feel good. It's weird to think that she's not going to walk back into Bartley Lodge ever again. Her life has been cut cruelly short, her body left out in the snowy fields.

My father is going to be distraught; he really did love Dawn. Perhaps in a way that he never truly loved my own mother. One thing's for sure, he will want revenge. He will be furious that the woman he loved has been torn from him in such a brutal way. He will be on the warpath for justice to be served. And with his own cancer diagnosis hanging over him, he's not in a good frame of mind. He may feel that he has nothing to lose. So it's possible he will be even more ruthless in his quest to punish his wife's killer.

That leaves me in a difficult situation, caught between loyalty to my wife and loyalty to my father. Either way, I'm going to lose one of them. There's no way forward that I can see that will allow me to keep both of them in my life after what's happened today.

My wife has been accused of murder. Do I think she's responsible? Honestly, no. Alicia is the most unthreatening person I know. The idea of her killing someone seems absurd. I just don't think she would do something like this. And she has no real motive. Dawn welcomed her into our family. In fact, Dawn was probably the person who welcomed Alicia the most. Alicia has no reason that I can think of to be on bad terms with Dawn, let alone to want to end her life. Unless there's something big that I'm missing...

Even so, how can I stand by my wife? I have to support my grieving, sick father, if only for my own ends. I also have to make my father understand I have no part in this murder whatsoever. I don't want him thinking that I'm somehow part of it. Or, even worse, that I'm some kind of accessory. I also need to make this clear to the police as well. Because Dawn's death has nothing to do with me. I'm certain that I will have to distance myself from Alicia so that I don't get dragged down with her.

It also becomes obvious to me I should use this as an opportunity to become my father's rock, his shoulder to cry on. As callous as it sounds, I have to turn this around so that he confides in me and trusts me. I can't risk losing everything I'm owed because of what's happened. Not when I have so much at stake.

Because the thing is, I'm in way too deep. I have debts stacked against my name. I've partied too hard and spent too much money on the drugs I rely on to get me through each week. Everything has spiralled out of control but there's nothing I can do to change it now. I owe huge amounts of money to people who aren't going to leave me alone until I can pay it all back, with a whacking great interest on top. The only reason they're leaving me alone right now is because I've told them I'm due a large inheritance from my father. One that will make all of my problems go away.

So I can't risk my father making changes to his will and reducing my share. I feel sorry for Alicia and I feel bad that she's got caught up in my complicated family. Perhaps one day I can make things right with her. She doesn't deserve this at all. But I have to look out for myself and save my own skin. Otherwise I'm going to end up in a much worse state than Dawn if I don't play things cleverly from here on.

I look up and I'm shocked to see Alicia through the glass in the lounge door. My wife is being pushed along the hallway; her hands still bound tightly. She looks straight at me. The expression on her face is like a dagger to my heart. Her eyes are big and pleading.

'Jack!' she screams, the terror palpable in her voice. 'Jack, tell them it wasn't me!'

I've never heard her so distraught. I stand up, but I stop myself from moving towards the glass that separates us. I don't know who really killed Dawn so there's nothing I can do to try to help her.

I shake my head slowly and, in that split-second, Alicia understands I'm not going to stand by her. Her legs immediately crumple beneath her and one of the officers has to catch her.

I look away. Alicia always saw the best in me. She believed in me. And look where that's got her. But I've got to forge ahead with the course of action I've decided on. I've got to save my own neck.

A few minutes later, a Garda officer sticks his head around the door to give me an update. My younger brother still hasn't been found. The sun has set for the day and darkness has fallen over the mountains. Ronan still hasn't been traced. He left the lodge with Alicia and she's been accused of murdering one person already.. If something has happened to him it will completely break my father, even more so than Dawn's death. Ronan has always been his favourite child, the son who is his spitting image. Seeing them together, people remark how alike they are. Like two peas in a pod. They share a close bond, one that I've been jealous of at points in my life.

Of course, if Ronan didn't return that would mean I'd likely get more of an inheritance from my father. The events of the last few hours are swirling around in my brain as I try to grapple with the order in which everything has happened.

It's safe to say this Christmas holiday is well and truly over.

My brother is missing.

My stepmother is dead.

My wife has been arrested for murder.

And I have my work cut out to try to keep my place in the family and my inheritance unaltered. There's a lot to do and to plan. So I best get started...

Chapter Thirty-Eight

Yasmin

My husband is missing. And Dawn is dead.

Bartley Lodge is swarming with Garda officers. Their handheld radios are crackling with static as the police inside the holiday lodge talk rapidly to their colleagues at the other end of the line. It's getting late and there's still no sign of them leaving and no further news of Ronan. The whole house is in chaos. Each member of the family has been moved into different rooms. I feel as though I'm being treated as though I'm guilty. Being shut up in my bedroom, unable to leave or speak to any of my family. I'm not even allowed to use my phone. Even though the officers have explained it's just so they can establish a timeline for the missing person, my husband, I feel like they're treating me like a criminal. And they've told us they will need to question us all when they're able to get us to a police station. In the meantime, I've been cut off from everyone while I go out of my mind with worry about where Ronan is and what might have happened to him.

Lily is crying again. It's way past her bedtime but she can't settle, not with all the activity that's going on in the house. She may be little but she knows something is amiss. I wonder if she's missing Ronan and if she realises that he's not here.

I pick up my little girl and cradle her, inhaling her sweet scent helps to calm my nerves. She quietens down and her breathing becomes more regular and then, finally, she drops back off to sleep. I don't attempt to put her back in her pram bassinet, which I'm using as a makeshift bed for her so she can sleep in my bedroom with me. I didn't want her across the hallway in her cot, I needed to keep her in my sight. Ronan's whereabouts is unaccounted for and we have a killer in our midst. So my motherly instincts to protect my daughter have ramped up to an even higher notch than usual.

I sit in my bed, my back against the headrest and my legs stretched out in front of me. Lily is snoozing on my chest. There's no way I'm going to get any sleep tonight but the closeness to my baby is comforting me. I've left the curtains open but all I can see is the bleak, foggy night. The stars are obscured by clouds and it's hard to make out much in the darkness.

Where is Ronan? He's been gone all day. I have a horrible feeling that something really bad has happened to him. He knows this area well, he's been holidaying in the Wicklow Mountains since he was a child. He's good with navigation and he is fit and healthy. So why hasn't he made it back to us?

Judging by the handcuffs around Alicia's wrists and the snippets of information I've managed to pick up on, as the Garda officers haven't exactly kept their voices down, the police suspect that my new sister-in-law killed Dawn. I couldn't believe what I was hearing at first, but it seems she was found by my stepmother-in-law's body. It sounds like Dawn was strangled and then left out in the snow. A grisly end for the poor woman.

Of course, Dawn played me for a fool. She used me when it suited her and then treated me like dirt. She was an obstacle to my relationship with Patrick and a recently a source of tension for me.

I'm not going to pretend that life won't be easier with her out of the way. It will be like rewinding the clock a few years. I'm going to go back to being the matriarch of this family, just as I should be. They'll all need an alpha female guiding them in the fallout of this Christmas. The trust of this family will be returned to me once more. I just hope Ronan returns – it could complicate my position if he doesn't. I also want him by my side in the next phase of our lives. He may have made big financial mistakes recently, but we can overcome them together. After all, he's the man I married and the father of my child. We're a team.

He has to come back, otherwise all of my plans are in tatters.

Alicia left the house with Ronan. So I'm sure the police think they might have a double murder on their hands because my husband hasn't returned. The longer he is missing, the more likely this possibility seems to be. Alicia seemed so nervous, so eager to please. I thought she'd be a complete pushover to manipulate and to manoeuvre out of the family. It seems I underestimated her.

If Alicia did do this, if she really did kill Dawn, then this is a two birds with one stone situation for me. Dawn is dead and Alicia will be carted off to prison. It would spell the end of her marriage to Jack. Both of my female rivals would be removed in one night. My place at the heart of the family will be restored once and for all.

I close my eyes and try to calm my thoughts. The notion that my husband might be dead is one that I'm trying not to contemplate. Every time the possibility enters my mind, I try to block it out. The idea of being a widow at my age, with an eleven-month-old baby left fatherless is too devastating to consider. I pray, for the first time in a long time, for my husband's safe return.

Chapter Thirty-Nine

Alicia

I'm sitting in the high-backed office chair; my whole body is trembling with cold and with fear. I've been allowed a toilet break, with two officers marching me to the bathroom and back again. I caught a glimpse of Jack sitting in the lounge as I was escorted back to the office. Only yesterday we were entwined together on the sofa and now I'm torn apart from my husband. Because when he looked at me, with that hangdog expression on his face, I knew he wasn't going to stand by me. He gave me a long, sorrowful shake of his head. My legs buckled from under me as the truth hit me at full force. Jack Silver has never truly loved me. I came to that realisation before I went travelling and I should've stuck to it. I should never have allowed him back into my life. Perhaps if I hadn't, I'd be on a sunny beach somewhere right now. But instead I accepted his marriage proposal, all because I wanted to believe that his feelings for me were as strong as my love for him. Tonight he's shown his true colours.

I've been in this room, unable to move, for at least fifteen minutes. The study feels stuffy and claustrophobic. This has to be a mistake. A nightmare that will quickly be put right.

I'm cursing my choice to come on this holiday. I could've said no. I could've stayed at home and not had to deal with interacting with the Silver family or getting caught up in their twisted family dynamics. I'm heartbroken at how this has all played out. My marriage is about to end before it's even started.

One of the officers has taken a bit of pity on me, as a silver foil blanket is draped round my shoulders and a hot mug of tea is pushed into my still frozen hands. It's my second lot of tea today and my head is still pounding from the caffeine I consumed earlier. But it's the least of my problems right now.

I take a gulp of the hot liquid and it scalds my tongue. It's not pleasant, but at least it jolts some feeling back into my body as the tea slips down my throat.

After what seems like hours, I hear a commotion outside the room I'm in. I hear shouting but I can't make out who it is. And lots of voices are fighting with each other to take control of whatever argument is happening.

'What's going on?'

Neither of the officers answer me.

Things go quiet. I'm left to my own thoughts, circling round and round. I have to make them believe that I played no part in the murder of Dawn Silver.

A more senior officer barges into the office, the door banging loudly behind him and the wail of a blue siren in the background.

'Mrs Silver?' the deep voice asks.

'Yes,' I croak out my reply.

'I've got some questions to ask you.'

My stomach drops and I know this nightmare is only just beginning.

***

The Garda police remove me from Bartley Lodge, from the luxury holiday home where I thought my life of wealth and happiness was just beginning. It takes several hours for them to drive me through the perilous conditions to the nearest police station. I'm put in a cell to begin with and told to get some rest. But there was no way I could sleep on that hard bed with the thin blanket. I've lost all sense of time and I have no idea how long I've been awake for. There's no natural light in this cell for me to work out if it's day or night.

Hours later, I'm asked if I want a solicitor in the interview room with me.

'No,' I say defiantly, 'I'm innocent, so I don't need defending.'

I'm taken into the too-bright white room. The questioning begins, thick and fast with no time to think properly. Two officers sit opposite me.

'Can you confirm your name is Alicia Silver?'

'That's correct.'

'And you were at Bartley Lodge on holiday with your husband Jack Silver and his family?'

I nod.

'Can you answer for the purposes of the tape recording please?'

'Yes, correct.'

'To state at the start of the recording, you have been arrested on suspicion of the murder of Dawn Silver. You do not have to say anything. But it may harm your defence if you do not mention when questioned something which you later rely on in court. Anything you do say may be given in evidence.'

'Understood.' My heart is beating wildly in my ribcage but I try to remain calm.

'And you've declined to have a solicitor present?'

'I'm innocent, I don't need a solicitor.' I repeat the same line I said earlier, although now I'm feeling less confident.

'If you change your mind at any point, let us know.'

'I will.'

I'm already starting to regret my decision not to have a solicitor. But surely I don't need one? Surely they will realise soon enough that I have nothing to do with this.

'So you were spending Christmas with your in-laws?' The man from yesterday with the grey eyes and grey beard is leading the interview.

'Yes.' My hands are shaking. I'm keeping my answers brief because I'm afraid I will say something wrong.

'It's not easy being on holiday with your in-laws, is it?'

I gape at him. It seems jarring for him to make a flippant comment like this. But I get why he's doing it. He's trying to strike up a rapport with me. I've watched enough crime series on TV to know that.

'And you're recently married?'

I nod and then remember the tape. 'Correct,' I croak. 'Jack and I married in October.' It seems bizarre saying this now. So much has happened in the last few days, my happy wedding day seems like another life.

'What happened after you left Bartley Lodge yesterday morning?'

'I had been paired with Ronan to go looking for Dawn—'

'Was that your choice?' The burly female officer cuts in now. I can tell by her expression that she doesn't want to spend time on chit-chat. She just wants to get her job done.

'Sorry, what do you mean?'

'Who paired you with your brother-in-law?'

'Um, well, I guess Jack did, in a way. Because he wanted to go with his father.'

'And why was that?'

Jack has let me down but I'm not about to tell them there was an almighty row between my husband and his father.

I shrug my shoulders.

'Do you know Ronan Silver very well?'

'Not massively. Jack and I only got married in the autumn. This holiday was an opportunity for me to get to know Jack's family.'

My answer is met with stony silence. The tables have turned.

I fiddle with my hands in my lap, looking down and trying to avoid the gaze of the Garda officer interrogating me.

'Do you know where Ronan Silver is?'

'No.' I hang my head. I get the feeling I may be facing a double murder investigation if Ronan isn't found alive.

Out of the corner of my eye, I see the older officer shakes his head very slightly.

'Are you aware that Dawn Silver was severely allergic to nuts?'

I blanche at this. Did my red velvet cupcakes somehow contribute to her death? I resolve to tell the truth.

'I'd made those cakes with almonds before you see, but when I gave them to her I didn't know she was allergic -'

'I see.' She cuts me off again. 'And do you regularly add almond flour when you make hot chocolate?'

My head is spinning and I just want to press pause on this interview. But they're far from finished.

'I think... I think I should stop. I'd like a lawyer before I answer any further questions.'

'Very well,' the bullish female officer crosses her arms and stares at me. 'We'll end the interview and continue our discussion later.'

I turn away, brushing my strawberry-blonde hair from my eyes and I try to think clearly. I'm exhausted. I'd give anything to be waking up in my home in London, far away from all of this drama. But the lovely flat is probably not going to be my home any longer because there's no way my fledgling marriage will be able to survive this. However much I love Jack, I can't forgive him for the way he looked at me back at the lodge.

I hope they find Ronan soon, for his sake and for mine. I'm not a killer and perhaps locating my brother-in-law might help me to clear my name. He was with me this morning; he can account for a large chunk of time. He can tell the police I didn't do anything unlawful. Although, given that my husband doesn't seem to be sticking up for me, I'm not sure if his brother will prove to be any more honest. I shiver with fear.

Will I go to prison for this?

And who really killed Dawn?

Chapter Forty
Early hours of December 26th
The Killer

After Jack's antics at the end of Christmas Day, I can't sleep. The late night gives way to the small hours and I lie awake thinking about everything that has happened on this holiday. And I burn with anger.

I've observed that Dawn has a habit of getting up in the early hours of the morning and going to the kitchen to get a glass of water, with ice. I listen, straining to hear the familiar tread of her footsteps. I hear a door creak, I sit up. It's her. And now she's padding down the stairs.

Cautiously, I inch out of bed. I'm still fully clothed. I follow Dawn downstairs.

As I step into the brightly lit room, I hear the familiar whir of the ice dispenser and watch as several cubes fall into the tall glass that Dawn has in her hand.

'Oh, hello. What are you doing up?' Dawn asks me. She's wearing pink fluffy pyjamas and matching fluffy slippers.

'Couldn't sleep.' I keep my answer as short as possible. I turn to the cupboard where the alcohol is kept. 'Fancy something stronger? Hot chocolate with Baileys?'

'Oh go on then.'

Dawn doesn't take much convincing. Everything is going exactly to plan.

I let Dawn jabber on in the background, talking about anything and everything. She doesn't even pay attention to what I'm doing.

'I've put a dash of cold water in, so it's drinking temperature.'

Dawn takes her drink willingly and sits down on one of the kitchen chairs.

'Happy Christmas,' I say softly.

Dawn echoes my words before drinking deeply from her festive-themed mug.

It happens quicker than I expect. Dawn's chatter fizzles out and her eye lids begin to droop. Before long, she's out cold, slumped back against the chair. She's so gullible. She had no idea that her drink was laced with strong sedatives along with ground almonds stirred into the drink mixture. She should've known better than to trust me.

The next part of my plan is going to be easy.

I head into the hallway and stand for a minute, listening in the darkness. There's no movement. The rest of the house is quiet.

I pull on my boots, gloves and thick coat and go back into the kitchen. I check Dawn – she's completely unaware of anything that's going on around her. I wind her bright pink scarf around her neck before sliding open the enormous bifold doors at the far end of the kitchen. The cold air hits me immediately.

I locate the big sack truck, now emptied of logs, and I roll it towards the open doors.

Dawn is bulky but I manage to manoeuvre her out of her chair, pulling her out of the doors and onto the sturdy truck. It takes some time but I succeed. Dawn is heavily asleep and completely pliable. I see her neck flushed red and assume the almonds are having the intended impact.

I drag Dawn in the sack truck, away from the lodge and over the nearest hilltop. My plan is to dump her just on the other side of the little crest that can be seen from the windows of Bartley Lodge. I want her to be near enough to be found.

It takes an enormous amount of effort but I've been working towards this day for a long time. I've been hitting the gym, lifting weights, ensuring that I could go through with this.

I tip this despicable woman onto the blanket of white beneath my feet. She flinches slightly as her body hits the hard, cold ground. I've got to do this now, before she wakes up.

First, I lay her out. I fan her hair around her head and position her limbs. She looks just like a snow angel. But this woman is anything but. The scarf is already around her neck, and she's still out cold. It doesn't take much for me to squeeze the life out of her.

Finally, it is done.

All that's left is for me to cover my tracks. Although, the snowflakes are falling so thick and fast again that mother nature will help me with that...

Chapter Forty-One
Epilogue
Alicia

I've had time to turn things over in my mind as I pace round and round in this police cell, going over the events of the Christmas holiday. But still nothing makes sense. I've been assigned a solicitor and I've had a chance to speak with her, to tell her what really happened before my next interview. I just hope it goes better with someone there by my side as I'm being interrogated. But I'm not sure if the solicitor is even convinced that I'm innocent. How am I to win a murder trial if the person defending me isn't behind me one hundred per cent? But she's all I can afford, so I've got no choice. She's my only option.

My cell door is opened and I'm ushered along a grubby corridor, back into the same interview room I was in just a few hours ago. My solicitor is already there and I give her a nod as I walk into the room. The questioning begins again, going over the same ground that was covered earlier on. My hands are shaking and I'm finding it difficult to focus.

'You said you didn't know the whereabouts of Ronan Silver?' the grey-bearded police officer asks me.

'No. He went ahead of me. I was slowing him down and couldn't keep pace with him.'

'And you didn't see him after that?'

'No. Has he been found?'

There's a pause and my heart leaps into my mouth. I'm frightened that something terrible has happened to my brother-in-law as well.

'He has been found. Alive,' the male police officer confirms and I feel all eyes on the room on me.

'Oh thank goodness!' I exclaim, genuinely relieved that Ronan isn't dead.

I listen as the female officer tells me that he made it to the village and had managed to stay in the pub for the night while the storm raged on. He provided me with an alibi for the first few hours of the day. He told the police he was with me for several hours after we set off from Bartley Lodge to look for Dawn. But he also told them he couldn't vouch for me before or after that stretch of time. My heart sinks.

I thought Ronan being found might result in clearing my name. But I was wrong. The Silver family have turned their backs on me. I'm sure that Patrick will believe that I killed his beloved wife; Ronan isn't prepared to protect me; Yasmin will be only too happy for me to take the fall and even my own husband has made it clear he isn't going to support me. The only person who might vouch for me is Zara. At least that gives me a glimmer of hope, however small. I need a straw to clutch, otherwise I'll go insane.

After another hour of intense questioning, I'm marched back to my cell. They haven't charged me yet, but I feel like it's only a matter of time. I wonder if anyone else is being questioned.

I know there's something that I'm missing. A piece of the puzzle that would help me make sense of the bigger picture. Someone wanted Dawn dead. And they set me up. For a few dreadful hours, I contemplate if it was Jack. Was it possible that he married me in order to orchestrate this whole thing? He and Dawn had a tense relationship. Perhaps he wanted to get rid of her and saw me as the perfect scapegoat to take the rap. But, after turning the idea over many times, I come to the conclusion that Jack wasn't behind all of this.

I've known Jack for a long time. He's squeamish when it comes to blood and I've never seen him raise his hand to anyone in all the time I've known him. I refuse to believe that my husband is a killer, even if he is weak. And I can't comprehend a world where he married me just to set me up.

Patrick has a cancer diagnosis so I don't think murder would be on his agenda right now. He and Dawn seemed happy together, and she was supporting him through a tough period in his life. He may have shown a temperament that's quick to anger but I think it's unlikely that he would arrange for Dawn to be killed or do the deed himself.

That leaves three possibilities. Yasmin had it in for me from the moment I stepped into Bartley Lodge. Her behaviour towards me was awful and she and Dawn had a strained relationship. I have no concrete evidence but Yasmin is high on my list of suspects.

I keep pacing round the small cell as thoughts whir round my brain. My brother-in-law Ronan left me on my own in the freezing cold, in treacherous conditions. The more time I've had to think, the angrier I feel about him abandoning me. Not only was it dangerous for me but it's also the reason why I have a chunk of time in the day unaccounted for – and so does he. He went missing for a number of hours, before being found safe and sound in the nearest pub. Yasmin and Ronan are two distinct possibilities but I have no proof, only suspicion.

Zara befriended me and she is the only person I might be able to reach out to for support. I don't think she would set me up but she also had a challenging relationship with her stepmother. I don't want to rule her out of my list of potential suspects but, as she might be the only person who can help me, I will concentrate on trying to unmask Yasmin or Ronan. Maybe, as husband and wife, they both had a reason to want Dawn out of the picture and so worked together.

Yasmin's interactions with Dawn were brimming with tension. If I can work out why, find a motive... It's going to be difficult, trying to dig into what really happened but it's the only thing I have to hold onto.

I have to find out who killed Dawn, I can't be sent down for a murder I didn't commit.

I'm innocent.

I just hope the police believe me.

Chapter Forty-Two

Zara

I did it.

It was me.

I killed Dawn.

I hate her. I've hated her since the second I met her. Eighteen long years I've had to put up with that woman. The person who took my mother's place and stole my weak father's heart. And that's not all she did. Dawn was a gold-digger. She rushed my father down the aisle and then took everything from him – and from me. She made sure she was the recipient of his estate. And then she engineered his tragic death. Then she caused the house fire that killed him.

So really, my actions are just evening the score.

I look out at the water and reflect on how it all came to this. The reality is, Dawn was never the bubbly, friendly woman she pretended to be. She was a cold and calculating killer and she deserved to die.

Alicia being part of this messed-up family just gave me a double reason for revenge. Because it's true that Alicia and I had been at university together. Not that she remembered, not properly. She recognised my face but she didn't recall the details, whereas I remembered it all. Every single moment. Alicia befriended the girl I had chosen to be my friend on the first day living in halls. She took Rosie from my grasp at the end of Freshers' week and they became a close-knit unit, sharing secrets and dreams together. That should have been me. It should have been my friendship and my life. Instead, Alicia came swooping in and ruined *everything*. And she was oblivious to the pain she caused me.

I found it hard to make connections when I was younger. I so badly wanted Rosie and I to be the best of friends. We clicked instantly and I felt like I could talk to her in a way that I hadn't been able to do with anyone else before. But Alicia, with her sugary sweet demeanour, stepped in my way. Instead of a university experience filled with friends and parties, I struggled to find my tribe. I became a loner, the girl who sat and ate her lunch on the park bench by herself, the girl who never got invited to anything. All because of Alicia.

When I left university, I wanted to put all of that behind me and to forget about it. Although, I named my canal boat *Petal* so I would never forget Rosie, my rose. I discovered I had a talent for drawing and became a designer. It was so freeing to finally find something I was good at.

I sigh. Life seemed to be looking up. Except, Dawn had entered my life in my mid-teens and turned everything at home upside down. She married my father and then rapidly stole his affections, poisoning him against me. When I went back home for short visits in my early twenties, I noticed the happy marriage facade that Dawn had created was slipping. Dawn and my father were arguing more and more. I remember one night, when my father and I had a rare evening to ourselves, he confided in me that he wanted a divorce. Within weeks of that conversation, he was dead. The police said the fire was caused by faulty electrical goods. But I knew it wasn't true. She did it. She killed my father.

My anger towards her has never faded. I pick up one of my sketches and rip it in half, letting the fractured pieces of paper flutter onto the floor.

After that, I went off the rails a bit. I found it hard to focus on my drawings and I felt lonelier than ever. My grief for my father was all-consuming. There wasn't anyone I could talk to about it and I spiralled into a deep depression. But then I remembered Rosie. I tracked her down on social media and discovered that she was working in fashion and we had a mutual connection through my design work. I engineered a meeting. We went for a drink together. I was so happy. I thought that this was our time to become the best of friends.

But I was so wrong.

Rosie spent the whole evening moping because she'd had a massive falling out with Alicia and they hadn't spoken for months. It was music to my ears, an opportunity for me to fill the friendship void. Except it became clear that Rosie wouldn't stop pining after her 'best friend' Alicia. I was so mad. I was determined that if I couldn't have Rosie, then nobody could. I went too far.

Unfortunately, Rosie died.

Flames licked the barn conversion she was living in and her home burnt down to the ground, just like my childhood home did. But I wasn't in Rosie's close circle of friends and the police never suspected me of being involved. That's what happens when you're a loner. You become invisible.

I don't know why Dawn insisted on taking me under her wing after my father's death. Perhaps she just wanted to keep up the pretence to the outside world that she was kind and caring. Or maybe she just didn't want me stirring up trouble regarding my father's estate. I resisted as much as possible in the initial year after my father's untimely demise. She was responsible for his death and I didn't want to see her face ever again. But then I realised I needed to keep Dawn in my life, to keep an eye on her and to plot my revenge.

Not long after my father passed, Dawn began dating Patrick. All of a sudden, she was jumping into another marriage and she cajoled me into becoming part of the Silver family. I was reluctant and I wanted to avoid becoming part of her extended family at all costs. But then I met Jack. He was kind and funny and listened to me. We struck up a friendship, purely platonic. I was ecstatic to have a genuine friend. We'd meet for after-work drinks in London and our message exchanges were full of the kind of memes that we both found hilarious. It was good to have someone on my side, someone who got me.

Things began to settle. I thought I'd be able to put the past behind me. Jack was my lifeline, as long as I had him everything would be ok.

Except, in a strange quirk of fate, Alicia popped up in my life again. She was determined to be in Jack's life, even though he didn't love her. He told me so himself. But she wouldn't let up, and she kept finding ways to infiltrate his social life until she wore him down. I hated her. She stole Rosie from me and, in some twisted déjà vu, she was stealing Jack as well. The worst part was Alicia didn't even acknowledge my existence. She was so focused on her own obsessions.

Jack and Alicia's wedding sent me over the edge. I only stayed for part of the day – I couldn't stand celebrating a matrimony that I knew Jack didn't believe in. He told me all about why he was really marrying Alicia one night at the pub when he'd had too many beers. I was his confidant. I loved that he trusted me with his secret but my jealousy for Alicia burnt bright. I decided enough was enough and I needed to do something about it.

So I set the whole thing up. I bided my time, just waiting for the right opportunity.

I'm not sorry for what I did. Dawn killed my father and I was just exacting my revenge. Dawn probably had similar plans for Patrick anyway, so I did the right thing. The best bit was framing Alicia. She didn't see it coming. It was tricky but I'd calculated the different reactions of each of the family members. When Dawn's disappearance was first noted, I spun the idea that she might have gone for a walk in the woods, knowing Patrick would want to search there. And I indicated to Ronan that he should search along the dirt track that dipped down to the village. It was 50/50 as to whether Alicia or Yasmin would accompany Ronan and discover the body. I guessed Yasmin would stay home with the baby and everything played out just as I wanted.

Finally, I've made Alicia feel all those things that I felt because of her: lonely, scared, frightened for the future. And when she's behind bars, I will have Jack to myself. Things can go back to the way they were. And, even better, Dawn got what she deserved too.

It's not the first time I've killed. And it won't be the last.

I'm not done yet. So many people have wronged me.

But, for now, Dawn is out of my life and I have Jack. He's my friend. And Alicia can't come between us anymore.

The police questioned us all individually at Bartley Lodge and they carted Alicia off in a police car first and then Ronan. The rest of us were able to return to our homes until further notice. In these hazy days between Christmas and New Year, I have stayed put on my canal boat, waiting for an update. No one has reached out to me since I left Ireland – not Patrick or Yasmin or even Jack yet. So I'm holding my breath, waiting to see what happens next.

As I sit, staring out of the window at the icy water that's currently frozen solid, I'm aware of the blare of sirens in the background. Every time I see blue flashing lights or hear the distinctive sound of a police car, I wonder if they're coming for me.

It's New Year's Eve today and I've covered hundreds of blank pieces of paper with my doodles. Then it happens. There's a loud knock on my window, making me jump in surprise. It's the police. They want to come in. I thought they'd call me first.

I hesitate.

But then I wrap Dawn's blood-spotted scarf that I kept as a memento of that night around my neck and slowly open the door to let the officers into the sanctuary of my little boat. Even when they see all the photos of Alicia on my cork board and find the hundreds of letters that I'd written to Dawn but never sent stuffed in my desk drawers, I remain calm.

I have no regrets.

Because, all in all, it was the best Christmas holiday I've ever had.

Extract: The Christmas Party

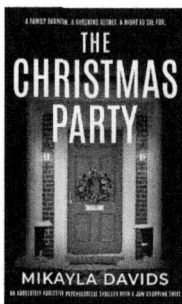

A FAMILY REUNION. A SHOCKING SECRET. A NIGHT TO DIE FOR.

THE CHRISTMAS PARTY

MIKAYLA DAVIDS

AN ABSOLUTELY ADDICTIVE PSYCHOLOGICAL THRILLER WITH A JAW-DROPPING TWIST

Prologue

I spin with my sister in the middle of the dance floor, our hands clasped tight, whirling round to the music just as we did when we were children. The DJ is playing yet another classic tune and we both shout along at the tops of our voices, smiles wide, eyes bright, mirroring each other. Rainbow-coloured disco lights shine across the vast room and the crowd around us shimmers and sparkles.

The moment I've been hoping for is finally here. After ten long years, my family are together under the same roof again. My two sisters, my mother, our children and our husbands. We're reunited after a decade of not speaking. But I don't want to think about the terrible night that shattered our family because I've waited for this day for a long time.

As the song ends, I stagger, wobbling on my high heels and putting a hand to my throbbing head. I feel a steadying arm loop through mine and I'm guided along the edges of the friends and family gathered here to celebrate in this exquisite hotel.

Everyone else seems to be in the moment, lapping up the festive atmosphere, but I'm on edge and I can't seem to let my hair down, despite the champagne that's flowing. Everything looks perfect on the surface. But, right now, I need to get away from the party.

When I exit through the double doors, the noise instantly dims and I feel like I can breathe properly again. I make my way along a winding corridor, my sister's hand in mine, and then we swing open another set of double doors into the grand foyer. This is the dazzling focal point of the building, with its curved marble staircase and sweeping gallery complete with a glittering crystal chandelier.

The first thing I notice is the strange silence. The sounds of the party in the background shut out by the soundproofing.

The second thing I notice is the dead body. Lying spread-eagled on the white marble floor, a pool of dark red blood surrounding the head like a halo.

I'm stunned, surely this can't be happening? But my sister inhales sharply next to me so I know I'm not imagining this. This is not a horrible dream. It's real.

My heart is hammering in my chest and my mouth feels dry. I lift my chin and make myself look once more at the person lying on the floor. I immediately recognise the broken figure at the foot of the steep marble staircase.

And I scream...

If you were addicted to *The Christmas Holiday* and you're looking for more festive thrills, then check out my novel *The Christmas Party*.

Also by Mikayla Davids

The Christmas Party: An absolutely addictive psychological thriller with a jaw dropping twist (The Bailey family psychological thrillers Book 1)

The Family Secret: A completely gripping psychological thriller full of incredible twists (The Bailey family psychological thrillers Book 2)

The Couple on Holiday: A completely addictive and gripping psycho-logical thriller with a heart-stopping twist

Dear reader,

I want to say a MASSIVE thank you for choosing to read *The Christmas Holiday*. This is my second psychological thriller and I absolutely loved writing this story. I had lots of fun plotting the twists and turns in this book! And I also enjoyed exploring the Wicklow Mountains setting. If you were entertained and would like to find out about my new releases, you can sign up to my mailing list: https://subscribepage.io/MikaylaDavidsBooks

Subscribe!

I hope you enjoyed *The Christmas Holiday*! If you did, it would be hugely appreciated if you could take a moment to write a review and post this on Amazon.

Leave a review!

I'd really love to hear your feedback, and reviews are so helpful when building momentum for a book and to help other readers find new stories. If you would like to get in touch with me, you can do so via my Facebook page, through Twitter or Goodreads.

All my thanks,
Mikayla Davids

Follow me on Twitter: @MikaylaDBooks
Follow me on Instagram: mikayladavidsbooks
Find me on Facebook: Mikayla Davids Books
Visit my website:
https://mikayladavids.wixsite.com/mikayladavidsbooks

Acknowledgements

This is my second psychological thriller and I had a blast writing this book! The setting and the characters came very clearly to me and I was eager to get this story out of my head and onto my computer screen! So my first big thanks go to my husband, who encouraged me to go off on a mini writing retreat while the creativity was flowing. My second thanks go to my parents and my in-laws who helped to look after my children whilst I was away for a few days writing the main framework of the story.

I also want to make it very clear in my acknowledgements that the Silver family are in no way based on my own in-laws! I have enjoyed many Christmases with my husband's family. And thankfully no one was murdered on any of those occasions!

But I did want to tap into a universal theme of going to spend Christmas in an unfamiliar setting and with a new group of people. Family comes in all shapes and sizes and the winter holidays are celebrated in so many different ways. I was intrigued by the idea of putting a new person in the mix of a complicated family dynamic and I hope I captured some festive feels along the way too!

Two of the characters in this story I've named after two of my grandparents – Alicia and Jack. Baby Lily's name is in honour of

Great Nan, who adored babies and was so loving and generous to my own children and they loved her just as much. The characters in this book definitely don't bear any resemblance to any real-life namesakes whatsoever! But I liked the idea of naming a few characters after family members who were much loved but sadly no longer with us.

I want to thank lots of people again for helping to make this book come to fruition. My mum for always creating lovely Christmases for our family and my dad for being an inspiration on how far drive, determination and a focused work ethic can get you.

I want to thank Lynne Haywood for being the best teacher anyone could have. You taught me how to think out of the box creatively, and this has been an invaluable tool throughout my adult working life, including the plotting of this novel!

A big thanks to my beta readers, all of your feedback is appreciated more than I can put into words and I owe you all a drink for your time and encouragement! A special shout-out to Angela, who has given much encouragement, as well as providing valuable insights from her own days in the police force. Huge thanks to my cousin Nicola, who has been an amazing champion. Thank you to my bestie Kim for reading, it means so much. Lots of thanks to Charlotte for help with admin and cheerleading! Rachel, thank you for all of your enthusiasm and for being so on it every time I've said, *'Could you just read this...'* And a massive thank you to Kelly Golden for all of your support and excellent feedback.

Thank you to all of my family, particularly to Rob, Kara, Lisa, Barry, Mark, Judy, Dennis, Linda, Clive, David, Ruth, Gavin, Zoe, Katie, Joe, Angelique, Corinne and all my extended family. I have so many happy festive memories with you all. And special thanks to Linda, my wonderful cousin and godmother, who also has a December birthday. When I was a teenager, to my parents' delight, Linda used to call or text me at five a.m. in the morning to let me know she'd already opened all of her presents and to generally share her joy of Christmas morning. My love of the month of December has definitely been down to your influence!

Thank you to Jade Craddock for your patience and kindness. Your work on this story has been hugely appreciated. Thank you to all of the wonderful book bloggers who have supported this publication, and a special thanks to Marnie from *Once Upon A Time Book Reviews* for giving me my first ever 5-star review!

My biggest thanks go to my two children. I love you both SO much and Christmases have just had that extra dash of magic with your cheeky smiles. I'm looking forward to the next one already!

And my final thank you is to every single person who has read this book. I'm so pleased that you've come along for the ride and I hope you enjoyed reading this story. I'd love to hear from you if so. And watch this space for future releases from me!

ISBN: 978-1-7392278-3-8

eBook ISBN: 978-1-7392278-2-1

Printed in Great Britain
by Amazon